SOME OF THEM WILL CARRY ME

TO ELIZABETH, FOR THE BODY AND THE LINE

Thank you to the editors who first published these stories: "Hangnails, and Other Diseases" online at *The White Review* (2017); "The Ethics of Piracy" in *BOMB* (2022); "Barbershop" online at *Granta* (2022); "A Triangle" online at *The New Yorker* (2022), "540i" in *Astra* (2022).

Art on cover:
Tschabalala Self
Two Women 3, 2021
Tulle, lace, velvet, thread, acrylic paint, digital print on canvas, and painted canvas on canvas
243.84 x 243.84 cm
96 x 96 in
Courtesy of the artist and Pilar Corrias, London
Copyright © Tschabalala Self

The publisher wishes to thank Edil Hassan and Sebastian Mazza.

Library of Congress Cataloging-in-Publication Data
Names: Scodellaro, Giada, 1988– author.
Title: Some of them will carry me / Giada Scodellaro.
Description: St. Louis, MO: Dorothy, a publishing project, [2022] |
Identifiers: LCCN 2022013903 (print) | LCCN 2022013904 (ebook) | ISBN 9781948980159 (paperback) | ISBN 9781948980166 (ebook)
Subjects: LCGFT: Short stories.
Classification: LCC PS3619.C58 S66 2022 (print) | LCC PS3619.C58 (ebook) | DDC 813/.6—dc23/eng/20220407
LC record available at https://lccn.loc.gov/2022013903
LC ebook record available at https://lccn.loc.gov/2022013904

ISBN: 978-1-948980-15-9

Design and composition by Danielle Dutton
Printed on permanent, durable, acid-free recycled paper in the United States of America

Dorothy, a publishing project books are distributed to the trade by New York Review Books

Dorothy, a publishing project | St. Louis, MO
DOROTHYPROJECT.COM

SOME OF THEM WILL CARRY ME
GIADA SCODELLARO

DOROTHY, A PUBLISHING PROJECT

CONTENTS

I would not mind
      if I were

                 a sinner,

but as it is
—let me assure you—
I sleep alone.

ALICE WALKER, ONCE

THE CORD

We met on a bus. It is not an ideal place to meet, the seats are too close, and everyone is ashamed to be there. To pause so often. When we met we were ashamed. In those too close seats, the blue cloth seats, I noticed his fingers right away, the clean cuticles. The fingers of men remind me of how they can be inserted. So I shifted the cotton, I lifted my hips. I grabbed his wrist. The pleats of my blue skirt moved against my thigh. Up. I guided the clean cuticles; I inserted them as we sat side by side on a bus.

He didn't wait for instructions, his fingers moved: the three that were free to roam or rest, the one that pressed against my clitoris, the last that moved inside.

After a short time the fingers were pulled away, out. He stood. He grabbed the cord with the same hand, the right hand, a ding, and the bus driver is pressing on the break with his right foot, and all the bodies are leaning forward, bodies on a bus jerking forward then slightly back in unison, another pause in our collective journey. And now I'm on the cord, and soon others will pull it, strangers will pull it, and some of them will carry me.

FREEDOM OF WHITE BOYS IN THE SAND

The girl was staring at the white men, the way their hair moved like the wind, too easy. In the middle of the busy field the girl called out to them, shouting obscenities. There were other people there too, a crowd of people, but it was the white men she had come to see.

The dirt shifted around the men and the crowd and the girl without discipline. All those standing in the field would later find the grains in the curve of their ears and on the tips of their eyelashes.

Emmanuelle came here every Tuesday afternoon to see them. It was her day off. There were only a handful of the white men left and they couldn't stop coughing. Their hair moved like the wind moved and she let her hands brush against their thighs.

Ambulances skipped along, howling in the distance as they gathered the dead and the almost dying. Birds made bird sounds; the crowd talked among themselves. The En-flamed Mountain hovered over them all.

The white men never paid attention to the girl, but she saw them as they walked and coughed and walked, shuffling their feet. She smiled at them sometimes, between her vulgar shouting, to see some acknowledgement from their bodies. But no, they could not pause, or hesitate. They were moving.

Unlike the white men, the crowd did notice the girl. Some were intrigued by her presence set against the yellow grass. They made up stories:

> *Maybe*, they whispered, *the girl is a widow who is tired of sleeping alone in a bed that is too large for her body, she hates rolling over in her sleep, you know, waking up alone, with her breasts askew, to that ever vacant side, a side devoid of any human chaos or warmth, so, so she's looking for a husband or a wife, someone whose ivory suits she can hang outside with wooden clothespins, a body she can easily dislike. Or, or maybe she's a ghost looking for the man who murdered her, murdered, she hadn't seen his face when he*

strangled her, only his elbows, so she is studying them,
studying all of our elbows to find him.

The crowd stayed on the paved road as they whispered about
the girl, close together in three straight lines, so the soles of
their shoes would not touch the yellow grass or the river or
the mud. The smell of lavender in the air.

They all wore the tailored three-piece suits, dark blue and
burgundy suits, gray and ivory suits. They felt more profes-
sional this way, even though the suits were not appropriate
for the climate, and they were not required to wear them.

The three-piece suits had been found floating in the
river, hundreds of suits. Those who discovered them found
them beautiful, it was beautiful to see all the colors swimming about, the dark blue and burgundy, gray and ivory. No
one knew if they were an offering from the Enflamed Mountain or a sign of a drowning.

No swollen bodies had ever followed the clothing, so after many days of debate the community decided to gather
them gently from the river and distribute them among the
crowd, and among the white men. They hung them with
wooden clothespins in their backyards. The breeze rolled

around the pants and vests and jackets as they dried, all of them dancing. The children watched the wind dress up and flail about, thinking anxiously about the day when their bodies would have to follow.

The crowd gave her a wave of their hand sometimes, or a nod of their head, *hello girl*. They presented her with their elbows. The girl noticed these gestures but didn't let on. Their bleached shirts were fastened tight around their necks, the collars filled with the day's sweat.

The white men are sightless, the girl thought. They could not perceive her or anyone else, they did not see the waving hands of the crowd, or the sleeves rolled up to reveal the elbows.

The girl bit her fingernails. Her hands were large, her fingers long. Her teeth snipping, clipping, clipping the nails, a repulsive habit. She bit them hard and fast, and she knew the white men would not notice this repulsiveness.

The girl's father had taught her that one must be consistent in one's oral compulsions. His had been the thumb, the men, and the cigarettes. Hers were the fingernails. He was dead.

The girl couldn't remember her father without the appearance of his thumb there, like a cloud. The right or the left thumb, or his cigarette placed between his full lips, or all three hanging around his teeth—*leftthumbcigaretterightthumb.*

Though it was not her real purpose for being in the field, the girl also looked for her sister amid the growing mob of people on their way home—for her sister's ears, which stuck out like splinters; or for her sister's nose, which was prone to bleeding; and for the trail of dots her nose would leave, the red red red, red; or for her sister's long oval nails, which once scraped the green-and-white wallpaper from their kitchen.

She looked up; she listened for her sister's laugh.

Emman's sister had gone out one warm night, 24°C, half-dressed, hair undone, loose, to purchase a helicopter. After a dinner of roasted scallops with lemon zest and Greek yogurt and pecorino, smoked sea salt, russet potatoes roasted with onions, with mushrooms sautéed in wine and butter, with rosemary, she left.

In June she left.

The girl wanted to fly too, of course she did, but she couldn't agree with this purchase. It was silly, irresponsible even, and she wasn't sure where they would put it. Helicopter fatalities were up by thirty-five percent. She told her sister so, *I'm not sure where we would put it, helicopter fatalities are up by thirty-five percent.* But the sister had convinced her that the helicopter was necessary now that their father was dead (their mother was alive, but had already left to be with a white man, John).

Think of the rotors, the sister said, *the thrust, to be able to land vertically, in a narrow space, or even the sound it would make, the crowd would look up at the sound, they would. Even the white men would look.**

---

*   And the yellow kitchen wall had glanced patiently, quietly, at the girl and the sister discussing the purchase of the helicopter. It could sense that a decision was close. Their voices were loud, but all voices seemed loud to the kitchen wall, so it did not know if it was a loudness that was suitable or one of anger. The thin curtains moved as the girl and the sister spoke of the machine. The kitchen wall had always hated these thin curtains—a suspended material that did nothing to conceal the sibling inhabitants or insulate the large windows, or keep the light out. The thin curtains obscured the view of the river. They were a source of endless torment and distraction. Soiled dishes, bits of scallop, rosemary, and potatoes stood waiting in the sink, and the thin curtains moved like the hands of anxious children. The sister continued explaining the benefits of the flying apparatus; she came close to the wall as she explained. Her mouth opened wide, wide like a cacao pod, and it stirred a feeling within the wall. It was a feeling that a wall can only have once, it decided, and it was true, the yellow kitchen wall would never experience such a thing again.

After a while the girl stopped looking for her sister in the sky. She wanted to look, but resumed staring straight ahead at the white men. But she still listened for the sound of the propellers, the whoosh of them, or for her sister's laugh. She might still be coming. The white faces were few and the girl heard only the birds wailing, and the wind, and the ambulances, the coughing, and the dirt accumulating bit by bit in her ear canal.

The girl's legs were tired from standing.

She imagined these white men (who exhibited the straightness of their teeth and the reach of their arms and the quiet of their noses) as little boys. White boys pushing each other hard with their fingertips, silver braces tightening, smoking, peeing everywhere, laughing, comparing the length of their penises.

The abundance of freedom must be thrilling for little white boys, she thought, and she remembered how as a child she used to swim with them in the river. The girl and her sister and the naked white boys as they played together in the sand—their butts even paler than the rest of their bodies.

In the field the girl took off her earrings, the wide hoops left behind by her mother. They had the appearance of gold, but when she dropped them on the ground in front of her, first one, then the other, they made only a small noise. Not enough to stir the earth, or the white men. They were not real gold.

Without earrings on, she thought, *I look like father.*

And she did, with her short hair and her hairy arms, Emman looked definitively like her father. But her father had once been a beautiful boy, one the other boys had been jealous of, and even the white boys had been jealous of him. They would stare at him for hours, so it was not an unfortunate thing to resemble him.

The girl was thinking of him and of the smell of tobacco on his thumbs when she fell.

It is shocking to be thrown to the ground suddenly, ridiculous even, and yet that's what happened to the girl as she dropped her mother's fake gold earrings and thought about her father. The girl fell hard on her left wrist and hard on her lower back, letting out two pieces of air, one of them a burp.

The girl was clumsy, but this particular collapse wasn't caused by her clumsiness. A boy was responsible. He was not one of the white men. He was a boy. He stood over her wearing a dirty ivory three-piece suit. The boy did not apologize for bumping into her, or for knocking her to the ground so suddenly, or for making her burp, or for any of the inconveniences that come with falling in front of a crowd. The crowd stared, and the girl stared at the boy, and the boy stared at the girl with confusion and what seemed like delight; the white men did not stare.

Her palms were full of dirt. The boy helped her up but did not provide her with his full strength (he really was no help at all), so when she grabbed hold of his small hands she still had to do most of the work to stand. The muscles in her legs burned, her knees spat.

While the girl tidied herself, the boy picked up the fake gold hoop earrings, putting them into his right pants pocket. He hoped she had not noticed this; he was a collector of things and wanted to keep them for himself.

The crowd was distracted by this collision—by this boy who chose to ride his silver bicycle home instead of walking, and by his dirty ivory suit, which should have been washed and hung to dry with wooden clothespins the night before. So even though they tried, the crowd could no longer stay within their three careful lines on the paved road. The soles of their shoes became covered with mud and they slid every which way—through the grass and up to the river and through the soil. They fell, everyone fell.

From the ground the crowd stared at the pair. The white men were troubled by the commotion, but did not stay on the ground, they didn't slow down and did not stare. From the ground some of the crowd was desperately intrigued by this event and by the way the girl bit her lip, and the way the boy touched his right pants pocket, and with the confusion that persisted around the field, the yellow grass. They made up stories:

> *Maybe*, they whispered, *she's found the right body to dislike in this boy, with his dirty ivory suit he'll fill the vacant side, and she won't have to fall asleep alone in a bed that is too large for her body, she'll be able to roll over in her sleep and wake up in the night to a side full of chaos, or warmth, and she'll have him pull on her nipples with his nails until the triangles of sun push through the thin curtains of the kitchen window.*

The others disagreed, *no, no, this ghost of a girl has finally recognized the murderous elbows, she'll feel obligated to create an olecranon fracture in them both, using a hammer or a wooden stick; she'll ruin his elbows.*

The crowd could see the weak outline of the gold hoop earrings in the boy's right pocket as it pushed against his thigh. They knew they would see the girl in the field on the following Tuesday. The new pair stared at one another, they touched each other's collarbones, and the crowd knew.

The pair left the field behind. They rode on the silver bicycle, traveling near the brown river where children were swimming and splashing. There were no white boys splashing, there were no white boys left. There were only the white men, who were beginning to get sick and would soon die—everyone knew.

The ride was bumpy; the silver bicycle hit many rocks and many pieces of gravel. The boy followed the instructions given by the girl who sat behind him; they made many turns. The girl had already forgiven the boy for making her fall. She could feel the bruises forming on her left wrist and somewhere near her lower back and buttocks. This was not the first time she had asked someone for a ride home. She delighted at the thought of sleeping with him.

The girl did not particularly care for his face, but she noticed that his hands were clean, tiny, and devoid of any calluses. The boy could feel her breathing on his neck and could smell the ivory soap on the girl and the lavender in the air. He began riding down an unfamiliar path with the Enflamed Mountain in the distance, red and hovering and ugly.

He hoped they might name the mountain after him one day, if he managed to do something heroic or memorable. He could be remembered for his stolen collection of goods, or for his soft unsoiled hands.

The girl held onto the boy's ivory suit and then began stroking underneath his un-tucked shirt, under his wife-beater, and onto his curved back. While she rubbed he began speaking to her, telling her a story about a talking fish and about preparing lentils for the new year. It was not meant to be funny, but she laughed, she felt it would be rude not to laugh.

They arrived at the home. It was old but beautiful and the color of a peach. The boy noticed the opened windows and a pair of thin curtains blowing in and out. The smell of the river reached them, the smell was strong, the boy thought this immediately, but he did not say it aloud, he felt it would be rude to say so. He thought it again and again: a smell like mud.

They took off their leather shoes at the front door. They went immediately to the bed, passing the kitchen, the thin curtains, and the yellow kitchen wall with its drops of red red red, red. The pair sat on the mattress. They laid upon the mattress with their bare feet on white cotton sheets. They rubbed their bare feet together. The boy told the girl about all the objects he had gathered over the years, so many of them, a large collection of items. This recounting lasted for hours.

The girl could not help her disinterest. When he paused to take a breath between the listing of watches and coins and hammers, she interrupted. The girl told him about her sister and the helicopter. She told him about her preoccupation with the white men, their thoughtlessness, their flat hair, and their inevitable extinction.

They talked to one another, but really only to themselves:

My sister's nose is prone to bleeding, you know, but helicopters are very safe, very safe, everyone knows this, but the white men do not, they don't know how to pay attention; that is why they are dying—

I like to feel the heaviness of the object, which is why I collect things. The weight of the watches and the coins, the jewelry and the perfume bottles, and for my hands to be filled with many objects at once. I try to guess their weight, and their value. My room is filled with such things, filled to the brim—

Of course I know they're safe, I know that they use helicopters in the wars, I imagine it's exhilarating to be aboard one, don't you? Think of the rotors, the thrust, to be able to land vertically—

And I hope to collect more things, to be known for this collection throughout the county, so the Enflamed Mountain might one day be named after me, I hope to be remembered for something, for anything really,

*for my collection of blue and white bowls, or candles,
or even for my soft unsoiled hands—*

*Imagine it, oh, the sound it would make, a safe sound,
the crowd would look up at the sound, they would.
Even the white men would look.*[†]

The boy pretended to care about these theories of the
white men, or the whereabouts of the sister, but could not.
He was distracted by the smell of the muddy river (which
reached him even here within the bedroom), and by the
girl's body, her breasts, her collarbone, and the smell of rot-
ting food, which escaped from the kitchen. He also thought
about his right pocket and the gold hoop earrings, which
hurt as they pushed against his thigh.

---

† The sound of their whispering and of their feet rubbing together could
be heard by the yellow kitchen wall, but it did not know that it was a
sound made by feet (the bed was just out of sight). And all voices seemed
loud to the wall, even whispering voices, even the sound of feet rubbing
together. The kitchen wall thought this sound, a familiar sound, was coming from the attic, or the bathroom, or from outside, beyond the thin
curtains. Maybe it was the sound of someone coming, a return, a flying
machine.

GEORGE WASHINGTON'S DENTURES

Like Deana Lawson's *Nation*, everything has value, even black materiality, even gold teeth, even spaces that resist authority—even the ceiling, or the corner of a bedroom, even the greased scalp.

BARBERSHOP

The brown hair was frizzy around her neck, and around her forehead there was some frizziness. Her ears held six piercings each and six earrings each, twelve. Her top lip was full, and her nose hung down almost to the full top lip, and the bottom lip was less full. Frozen, her profile was frozen, and the toothpick between the uneven lips, a branch between the lips. A blue plastic bag was wrapped around her neck, billowing behind her like a cape. Her top came so low it seemed as if she was wearing nothing except this blue plastic bag.

The diner window showed her profile, her neck, the plastic bag behind her, the collarbone. The top was concealed by the wall and the restaurant siding. Her face was in the big big window. The hot sauce was being poured over everything: the fries and the chicken, the grits and the grapes. The maple syrup was being poured over everything, over the fried meat.

The waitress carried a jug of water. This woman drank gallons of water the way her skin was. A swan. On her head a hive. When she laughed her head bent back.

And her eyes were everywhere, her eyes traveled, they caught the whole room, and she made eye contact with the person across from her, with the waitress and with the manager. She ate cherries and grapes two at a time, spitting the seeds into an ashtray. When she ate she let the toothpick fall to the table. On her tongue there was a tongue ring and a cherry pit. The seed. Gold hoop earrings.

Around her the diner seemed to be falling apart; the walls were stained. The counters were stained and the floors were stained. The aprons were stained with sauce and grease. The forks were not thoroughly cleaned. The flowers were drooping and dying.

She dipped the tip of her cloth napkin (blue and white, checkered) into the glass of tap water (which contained lemons and limes, sliced grapefruit), and she wiped the top and bottom lip. She kept the damp material over her mouth, her eyes moving all around. For a while her mouth was unknowable, covered by material. Near the glass of water a cup of iced coffee or iced tea, a brown liquid.

Next door to the diner was the barbershop with its wood paneling and a poster of men. The poster showed different hairstyles—some of the men were looking up, some were looking to their right with their profile showing, or holding their chins down. On some the faces couldn't be seen at all, just the back of their heads and the work of the clippers. Some hair was shorter, some longer. Twenty-eight styles total. A calendar on the wood-paneled wall showed October, the corner folded over to conceal the year.

When she finally removed the napkin from her lips, crumpling it all up and placing it back on her lap, she used her hands to speak. She rotated her wrists, she clapped her hands, she held up two fingers, then four, seven, she clapped her hands together, punched one hand into the other, the right punching into the open palm of the left, as if to emphasize something. Open, punch, wave, punch, clap, punch. Then she rubbed her hands together, as if moisturizing them or disinfecting them, caressing, and the rings were eight, none on the thumbs. She moved so often and so thoroughly that her body became a blur, the fullness of the top lip couldn't be detected, the blurry bun, the nose, the neck.

A blurry child grabbed onto her neck. The blurriness couldn't hide the fact of this small being. He grabbed at her. This woman was generous with him. The child's ears like her ears, the top lip the same, full, the frizzy hair. There had been placenta between them. They each wore a blue plastic bag around their neck; their backs were made of blue plastic. It was enough to drive anyone away.

A TRIANGLE

I saw the couple out of the corner of my eye. I noticed them as I stepped out of a medical building. I noticed them because everything else in my peripheral shifted but they did not. The wind was blowing the leaves, the leaves were dying and leaping, and the couple was so still. The couple was unmoving. I was too, looking at them. So it was the three of us as everything else moved, constant and full and wide. People brushed by our shoulders, sweeping our sides as they inched toward their destinations. People were busy. People didn't care about the couple standing in the middle of the uneven sidewalk. People stirred around them like the sea, splashing against their ankles.

The man held her arms, his manicured fingers grasping hard.

Near the couple there was a burnt chair: garbage, darkened wood, charred remnants. That's what had attracted my attention while leaving the building, the medical building, with the activated charcoal in my teeth—an abandoned chair all broken at the hips.

I imagined the impulse of someone purchasing a new chair, deciding to throw this old one away—picking it up with their knees bent and their lower back engaged, a contraction in the abdomen, separating it from their other possessions, and this object (made only for laziness or rest or gathering) being moved down a flight of wooden steps, being carried and offered to this sidewalk, sloppily, an old chair left to perish, and I imagined too the person who might have burned it, probably a man (men expect things to have violent ends) with a lighter or a match and the smell of cigarette on his thumbs.

The dead chair was near the unmoving couple.

There was a balance there I found significant, so I looked back and forth between them for six minutes, or seven. I knew the couple must have liked one another. They stared like children and kissed on the corners of their lips, and I knew.

If I followed the couple home it was because of her hair.

The building they entered was severe: red brick, steel,

iron, and glass. Ugly. I waited to see what would become of them, now that they were inside a familiar place.

Time passed and it began to rain. I thought of the burned chair sitting outside the medical building, the consequence of this location, its wooden frame peeling.

When the light turned on in the fourth window from the right, on the second floor, I felt relief. I became aroused. There was sweat, sweat on my nose, and my bowels were ready. There was water—the rain that was still coming down and the sweat that was still coming.

We were a triangle.

In the fourth window from the right, I saw pieces of them: the corner of a yellow painting, a bookcase filled to the brim, the light fixture, the tip of a houseplant's leaf, a purple sofa, the blue walls, and then finally, *finally* her face in the window, her hair, her closed eyes, his hand wrapped around her neck like a scarf.

Hers was a plain face, really, as unremarkable as a piece of furniture. A face marked with freckles.

She had the most average of lips, the dark right eyebrow, and the left just as dark, long eyelashes, a nose with a bump in the middle as if it had been broken in childhood, the freckles covering her cheekbones like sand, and her resting eyelids.

I couldn't see her eyes.

So I waited to see how long she would stay, unsmiling. The rain fell hard on my hands.

Her skin, her hair had distracted me.

It was the curl of it on her neck and on her forehead, the way it looked like a question mark, circuitous and pleading. It was the hair that had caused me to follow, to walk closely behind and wait on the street as they shuffled for their keys, the locks clicking and unclicking, their wrists turning, pressing their shoulders into doors, stumbling in, laughing, her name being called, *Cannella*, it sounded like *Cannella, Can*—cursing, letting the door slam, fast, fast up the flight of stairs, taking two steps at a time.

It made me stay longer than expected, and the rain wouldn't stop. The rain continued. It felt heavy on my shoulders, and it rose. I could feel the water reach the back of my knees, a flooding.

I did not think to leave, instead I walked back and forth in it, in front of the red brick, steel, iron building, her building, and in the middle of the street, which now looked like a swamp.

The gathering water rose to my thighs. It smelled of things in the moment before their dying. Invisible objects moved near my shins—empty condom wrappers and large pears and extension cords, wet books full of soft paper (paper like cotton), nail clippers, peppermints, plastic spoons, dead mice, jars of unopened whipped honey. Rising water. This flood wasn't like the ocean, but I pretended that it was. I kicked my legs. Waves formed, the current was taking me and the rain wet my hands.

Floating, I looked at the fourth window from the right. The couple resembled a photograph, so still, the man's manicured hand, his beautiful hand on the neck of the woman, her eyes shut, and her dark eyebrows reaching up in mild surprise.

I don't know how long she stayed like that, unmoving, but we must have been a sight to see—the current pulling against my ankles, the thunder, me almost submerged, but looking up, up, staring at the glass, at this person with the closed eyes and the imploring hair, the neck, freckles everywhere, skin like a burnt chair.

THE FOOT OF THE TAN BUILDING

A woman jumped from the top floor of a Northeast Bronx building, from the 33rd floor of a building, at around 10:40 in the morning (10:40 AM, a time that seems too early to jump from anything at all). The woman might have recently lost a child. The photograph online shows the body at the foot of the tan building, near a patch of grass. Under a white sheet—a waiting body. Before the woman's final decision she might not have considered the possibility of this white sheet, its thinness, or how it would not cover her body fully, the birds moving around her, how her legs would peek through at the bottom, her running shoes exposed, her childlike ankles exposed, and the woman certainly would not have considered someone taking her photo, this photo now posted online for anyone to see, capturing her ankles exposed in such a way.

THE BALCONY

Serendipità eats the watermelon alone. The whole melon, she cuts into it alone and halves it alone, she digs in. She makes bright pink squares, she digs them out with a knife and a spoon, and whenever the juice accumulates she tips the thing and drinks what she can. When she takes breaks from eating, she covers the flesh with a paper towel. Her fingers are covered, and when she's ready to begin again, she does so greedily, the light pink paper towel set aside.

The balcony is covered in green mesh netting; it isn't safe to sit on. Construction is happening throughout the home, there are wooden ladders about, nails, tarps, a saw, and on the floor white dust. The pipes are exposed and the wiring is exposed. The yellow building exterior and the brown shutters are covered with green safety netting. The church bells ring.

When it comes time for the construction workers to begin, Serendipità moves to the balcony. She carries the white dust under the soles of her bare feet, it's useless to sweep it, the white dust accompanies her.

It isn't safe to sit on the balcony, the one hundred construction workers tell her. She defies them. When draped across the balcony, Serendipità tries to make herself as light as possible. She holds her breath or breathes slowly, lightly. Also, she doesn't move much or at all, only to scratch an eyebrow or a forearm, or to look down at the traffic lights. It doesn't seem entirely dangerous or unreasonable for her to be out there on the balcony. If she can make herself light, it doesn't seem unreasonable. She chooses one position to hold while on the balcony, and she remains in this position for the next eight to twelve hours. Behind her there's the clamor of work.

And across the street a man in a white t-shirt is cooking. Serendipità can't see the food being prepared, only his moving arms, his elbows in a cutting motion and a grating motion. He seems skilled, practiced. His knuckles are bent. In this kitchen across the street there's a rotation of strangers, different people occupy the space, a cast of characters. Today it's this man in the white t-shirt cooking.

Downstairs, on the street and on the sidewalk, there are empty chairs and empty billowing tablecloths. The backs of the chairs are made of a wicker or straw material. Outside, it's windy. There's the smell of fresh paint; church bells vibrate.

On the balcony she eats the tepid watermelon. When the construction workers come close to the balcony she pretends to sleep. They admire her buttocks. With one eye open Serendipità notices someone new across the way—a woman. The man in the white t-shirt is gone and a crocheting woman has taken his spot. A shadow of the woman's hands is moving on the appliances, fastidious hands, knotting and unknotting. The hands are not old or new, they're just hands, there's nothing special about them.

Below, the crosswalk signs flash and beep, a countdown to pedestrian safety. But there's no one outside; at this time people are in church or in their kitchens. Serendipità consumes raw things and sits on her balcony.

The distant bounce of a basketball, a hissing, a kite in the air, all of the sources unknown. Finally, a man walks across the street below her (the mass ended), his eyes closed, his chest exposed and his white chest hair. Above, the sky: pink and blue and purple. On the balcony there's a plant with small leaves. The sound of construction. There's exhaustion in the sound, even laziness, and a sense of general melancholy among the construction workers. The closed-eyed man makes it to the other side.

Serendipità goes to grab her wallet, to get the cash. On her way through the apartment, she touches a woman's lower back; to get through the mass of construction workers she touches a man's elbow. The bedroom is dark, pitch black, the curtains are drawn but she knows the room well and finds the money easily—in the second dresser drawer, on the right, underneath the third folded cashmere shirt, in a small wooden engraved box. Serendipità distributes the funds. She opens the front door, she closes the heavy door behind the workers, and she curses under her breath, a *fuck* or a *motherfucker*.

There doesn't seem to be progress. There are new holes in the ceiling and in the walls, and a container of off-white paint is left dripping and unsealed.

Serendipità goes back to the balcony where it's cooler. An hour has passed since she gathered and distributed the funds, and since the hundred workers exited the property. The sun's almost gone. Across the street where the man with the knife cuts things and the woman with the hands crochets things, someone is now hanging items of clothing from a clothesline: wet jeans, wet t-shirts, pink shirts, blue shirts, lavender shirts.

Serendipità feels the balcony move beneath her and goes back inside. She gathers the watermelon rind. She throws everything away. She sweeps the floors. She mops the floors with warm water and white vinegar. She goes to the pitch-black room and waits for sleep to come.

Serendipità is on the balcony. On Tuesdays the view is the sea. There's nothing else, only the sea. The building across the street is gone—the man with the knife gone, the clothes-line gone, the crocheting woman gone. She likes Tuesdays best. The one hundred construction workers won't be coming to make their clamor; she will be alone. She's alone. She makes do with what she has stocked in the cabinets, and in the refrigerator, and in the deep freezer. Serendipità goes to the garbage. From the black bag she takes out some of yesterday's watermelon, she rinses off the white dust, takes it to the balcony. She eats the old watermelon, now dark red and hot on her tongue, sour. The sea moves, the sea moves and the boats make geometric lines, the lines come in and out.

Serendipità slathers herself with sunscreen, rubbing it in. Rubbing it even into her belly button. She pulls the red and green lounging chairs from the storage closet, one for her, the other for the plant, and they lounge. On Tuesdays the church bells are nonexistent, there's only sea and sky. Clouds. There's relief, and this relief can be seen around Serendipità's mouth. The sun is moving on the water like strobe lights, the clouds are moving on the water like traffic, small rocks roll in the breeze. In the distance—an inactive volcano. The water moves like a king-sized sheet on a clothesline. Seagulls are moving. The balcony is reflected in the water, and so is the green mesh netting, the plant, the yellow building, and the brown shutters. The weather on Tuesdays is hot and humid.

Serendipità strips down to nothing. Three moles are visible: on her right breast, on her right inner thigh, on her top lip. Stretch marks on her right breast, on the right inner thigh, on her calves. Tomorrow she'll purchase stamps from the post office. Tomorrow there'll be lines of people gathered at the post office.

An airplane moves overhead, drifting low toward the southeast. On Tuesdays airplanes weigh more and they fly with difficulty. On Tuesdays there is more travel and more birds. On Tuesdays it is cheaper to fly. The money's wrapped in rubber bands and nestled in the engraved wooden box in the bottom drawer. Rolled up hundred dollar bills. On the balcony it smells of the sea, of fish, and of coconut sunscreen. A ferry is moving slowly but begins to approach the port. A woman can be seen hanging over its edge, her body hanging over the white railing. Her black slides seem large, a men's size eleven or twelve; she wears no socks. Her black hair tumbles around her face. As she looks down into the water, one foot lifts up behind her, her hamstring pulls, and above her swollen ankles her dark skirt moves in the wind.

What Serendipità wants most of all is seafood. She craves it on Tuesday—grilled oysters, octopus (cut and grilled and charred)—and with lemon, seafood doused with lemon juice.

Serendipità stands in front of the deep freezer, the refrigerator, and the cabinets rummaging for shellfish, white wine, lemon. From the refrigerator she pulls out the octopus, the caviar, the capers, the bag of lemons.

It's important to eat from the sea on Tuesdays. She doesn't go to church, she never will again, but she devotes herself to food preparation. In the living room the ladders and equipment are gone but there's always evidence of labor in the holes, there's always a hole. The sun is setting.

Serendipità goes back to sit on the balcony while waiting for the food to cool. She thinks about the circumstances of the octopus, and its ink.

Serendipità is tanned (except for the stretch marks that span her body). She washes the appliances, the pans, in hot water, and the dozens of lemons are put back into the refrigerator drawer, the batter, the butter, the olive oil in the pantry, the sauce, the parsley put back into a vase. When she drinks sparkling wine the sun is gone. At this hour the sea can be heard but not seen. Outside it's pitch black and in her bedroom it's pitch black. The waves crash, and alone in the kitchen she eats what she has prepared.

Serendipità is allergic to lemon, so afterwards her throat, lips, and gums are swollen and bleeding. Afterwards, swollen and in the dark, she waters the plant.

After the sea there is silence. Things go about as they normally do—the holes, the plant, the parsley in its vase—but there's no sound. The man across the street slices something silently (maybe apples), no church bells, no beeping cross-walk. No banging from the one hundred construction work-ers, no rustling from the leaves of the plant on the balcony.

This is the day Serendipità prefers. On the silent day she exits her apartment early, moving down the stairs two at a time, jogging into the courtyard, and then out into the dry street. On the silent day the weather is dry, humidity prom-ises sound so there is no humidity.

The post office is always packed on the day of silence and it's packed when she arrives. It's an ideal day to confront the tasks presented by a post office: no one complains about the lines, or about the post office workers, or their temperament, about the temperature of this federal space, or about the cost of a stamp ($11). They can complain but they choose not to. In silence they wait in line. Behind her and in front of her—women. There are only women standing around in the post office. The women fan themselves with their packages; they move their body weight from one leg to the other.

When Serendipità arrives at the front of the line she orders special edition stamps, three sheets of twenty. She chooses the stamps with black people's faces on them. On a piece of paper she writes and hands over to the teller: *three sheets of twenty special edition stamps, black faces only, please.* When she's done she walks the long way home.

No cars honking. No ambulances. No barking and no crying adults. No echo or wind in your ears.

After the post office but before returning home Serendipità stops at the bakery, the fish store, the ice cream parlor. She writes down all the things she wants on pieces of paper: cannoli, cento grammi di branzino, red grape sorbet. She hands the slips of paper to the cashiers. Everyone is outside, quiet. She picks flowers outside the ice cream parlor. Serendipità wears a shirt that sends a message—Dr. King in swimming trunks, the sun on his face and on his suprasternal notch, the rest of his body in shadow and surrounded by pool water.

At dusk she wastes time watching the traffic light change from red to green to yellow, standing on the corner for an hour looking at her building from below, at her balcony and all the green mesh netting. Then she returns home. At home she does things she wouldn't do on a noisy day—lip synching, stretching, also mouthing vile things, being generally profane. In the silence she worries about the ongoing construction.

On the balcony the shadows move. Across the street the wind lifts a white sheet hanging from the clothesline, a big white sheet. Serendipità soaks the dried cannellini beans overnight to prepare for company.

After the silence there's company. One of the workers isn't prepared—no tools, no helmet, taking innumerable breaks, smoking breaks, and eating things from the refrigerator without asking. Serendipità finds her on the balcony, sitting down. She doesn't reprimand her, but they both know she shouldn't be out there, and that she shouldn't be sitting. They sit together. Serendipità doesn't know the worker's name. While the others bang on the walls and ceilings, they sit together. They feed each other anchovies from a can. The others stand under the red ladder with dust on their arms, with dust on their construction boots, their helmets.

After the silence there's company. It's a day for company. They come over in large groups. They drink tea, they discuss politics or the latest societal scandals, the weather. It's festive and slow. The one hundred construction workers are there, working around the festivities (except for the one construction worker who isn't working and isn't prepared).

This is Serendipità's least favorite day; she doesn't like gatherings or small talk. She's in a black dress, velvet. She wears earrings that touch her shoulders. A large part of her back is exposed, a large v of skin, and the muscles in her back move as she moves to pick things up. She sometimes moves to the pitch-black bedroom to rest. After the day of silence the talk of this day burdens—piercing laughter and lipstick on teeth.

The company leaves without Serendipità seeing them out.

(There is a day that cannot be commented upon. It exists and it consists of an extension cord, grape jelly, and hominy grits.)

On the day all the hair is removed Serendipità is pensive. She likes this day, not as much as the day with the sea, not as much as the day of silence. On this day she takes a bath. With lavender oil, peppermint oil, rose water, with differently sized candles nearby, the Bible nearby. After, she covers her body with more oil but also with lotion, creams, body butter.

She goes out. In her shortest dress, with her arms bare, her scalp bare, she wears no makeup. Her bald head feels cold when the wind comes by. She sits on a park bench. Very few people are outside, a handful. They also wear their skimpiest attire, their arms bare, they wear no makeup. It's a day for exposure, but most don't take the chance. Most do not dare. Despite the lack of pubic hair, and none inside the nose, none in and around the anus, most don't dare. No eyebrows, no eyelashes, no false eyelashes. It's a day meant to cleanse and expose.

On the day all the hair is removed Serendipità sleeps with Raven. They meet on the balcony with the green netting. They take turns straddling, filling, pushing—pushing a neck. They sleep on the balcony. For Raven it's an act of rebellion; for Serendipità it's something else entirely. An erect middle and index finger, both women are hairless, soft. Tonguing, Serendipità looks at the crevices in the apartment wall. Serendipità wears a diamond necklace and hanging diamond earrings. The jewelry clatters as they circle. The wind is on their abdomen. Raven opens her mouth and the silver fillings show. The saliva lands in Raven's open mouth. The plant sits nearby.

On the day the hair is removed Serendipità's father calls her on the landline. She listens on the receiver but doesn't speak a word.

In the morning there's fire—a few objects must be chosen (three) to be added to it. In the morning Serendipità's hair is long. Serendipità has no feelings about this day; she's indifferent. She chooses the objects (three) and moves to the heavy front door. She moves down the stairs, to the courtyard. The one hundred construction workers follow. She joins the crowd of humid boisterous hairy people on their way to burn things. In the distance, smoke. Serendipità looks for Raven. The walk is long and the crowd is thick.

Serendipità listens to the chatter: *and? no, no, the children are growing so what do they need with a child's toy? jazz; the jasmine should be replaced with arborio; glass jars of tuna in olive oil; braided it with beads at the ends, beads, yes, bees; a box with seashells glued to the outside and a guitar; baby's breath, purchased a nose, a hammer to the nose; the shears; the sheer dress with the long sleeves; an earring; an owl.*

The burning is quick, it's the walking that takes too long. When she's close the fire is not so hot against her face and her neck. Against her knees the fire is warm, on her ankles the fire burns. She throws the objects in one at a time, thinking about Raven's elbows. Serendipità burns the items that were handed down to her; she still owns so much. The people who have nothing to burn are allowed to give a small part of themselves—sometimes hair, sometimes fingernails, skin, one third of an organ. There is chatter and crying around her. The fire feels hot against Serendipità's back, her wrists.

On the balcony Serendipità listens to the ninety-nine construction workers as they return and get to work. She misses the sea, even the objects (three). She doesn't miss Raven or her father. On the balcony she combs her hair with a wide-tooth comb, she detangles it with olive oil. The smell of smoke is all around her as she detangles, sprays, combs through, pulling out a cluster of knots. Dead hair is all over the balcony, split ends all over. The crowd is thinning, and from this height she can see the few who have yet to offer parts of themselves. Far off a piano is played, the scales. Some people hesitate and a part must be forced from them.

There's so much hair on Serendipità's head, an unbearable amount. Serendipità parts it into twos, then into fours, sixes, eights. She braids quickly and without thought. Her arms ache. The hair reaches far down, but she doesn't like her hair to hang around her body, so the eight braids are tied up into a bun, that's all.

The ninety-nine construction workers crowd onto the balcony with Serendipità even though they know it isn't safe. The green mesh moves.

The workers try to intimidate Serendipità; they want a raise. The exterior of the yellow building is layered with green. Every week she's strong-armed into a new arrangement with them, into more benefits or higher stipends, more perks, more paid time off, a provision to work remotely. Nothing is quite repaired or constructed. The holes in the walls are getting larger and the white dust rests lightly upon her braids.

LEAVE A FINGERPRINT, GNOCCHI

boil the potatoes until soft, 1 kilogram
remove the wet skin, peel, dry, wait until cooled
smash the potatoes together into a paste, with your palms,
move your knuckles,
make a mountain of them and place a hole in the middle
put one whole egg in the middle
introduce the 300 grams of flour and the one whole egg into
the mountain of potatoes
knead until dough is formed
let sit
roll into long ropes, cut into small pieces (it is my favorite part)
use your fingers to flick the dough, usually with your thumb,
make an indentation, don't use a fork (it is lazy) leave a fin-
gerprint
boil water, the small pieces float, remove remove remove
serve, eat immediately

THREE MONTHS OF BANANA

The passport could not be procured. The women would not be seen by the administrator, or by his supervisor, they would not. When they asked for someone of authority they were ignored. They had filled out the application form, provided payment, submitted the accompanying documents: the birth certificates, the naturalization certificates and/or the proof of birth abroad, the state-issued identifications, the baby pictures, and the baby hairs. But they would not be seen, not now. They sat, waiting. The chairs were not comfortable, intentionally so, but they tried to get comfortable. The others walked up quickly, received a stamp, left with the burgundy passports in their pockets, well on their way to lands and/or seas. The women crossed their arms against their bosoms, their legs bent and crossed one over the other. The women watched these others come and go. The woman sitting near the wall sat low, with her neck on the back of the chair, looking at the ceiling and at the one window. The government building was in ruin. The paint was chipping, yellow paint with green undertones. A ringing phone went unanswered. The air was cold. There was the one window and its glass that showed blue, a cloud. The pair did not know how long this would take, they had brought snacks: rosemary crackers, yogurt, tangerines, string cheese, blackberries, seared scallops. Also sanitary napkins, floss. This was bureaucracy in action. It was plain. While they waited they were allowed the use of the restroom. They took turns. When they were emptied and still, they spoke:

See, Yvette?

What?

See? There.

What?

The glass, that part of the glass in the window, see how chipped it is?

Yes, I think I see—

Well, that's a shame. This is *all* a shame.

Yes. (pause)

And I can feel this damned wind coming in, from the crack, can you feel it? (pause) You don't feel it? I feel it right on my forehead. The air is coming in from the crack, right there, see, that hole right there? It's so damn windy in here, and there's only one window, and the only window in the place is broken, how about that, and why not open it up and let everything in?

Should we open it?

No. No, but someone should, someone might as well open it. It's really something, this place, and this damned window, it's practically wide open already.

Yes.

Wide open, it is. (pause) Wide like Betty's mouth (laugh), remember Betty Davis? Betty? Betty Davis with her mouth ajar, or Mabry, Betty Mabry with her mouth ajar, Mabry, no, it's Davis, I should call her Davis, Miles didn't treat her well, he didn't treat women well, did you know, for a year he treated her badly, and twenty years her senior, the name Davis belongs to her, I'll call her Davis, but do you remember that photo of her with her bottom teeth showing, her right breast leaning into the center, remember? In *Vibe* with her legs apart? How could you not? It was in *Vibe* or *Ebony* or something, you don't remember her straddling the motorcycle in the (sucks teeth), the zebra-print leotard and those sheer stockings, the fingers all painted red, a dark red, not a light red, a dark red, and her hair reaching up high, with all that metallic eye shadow and the opened nostrils, her shoulders covered with feathers?

Um, I don't think I remember that—

Well, that's what I wished to look like, like Betty Davis with black feathers on my shoulder blades and white-and-black leather boots (laugh), and when she whines, ooh, when she whines from the gut and she yells about fucking, oh alright, excuse me (laugh), sorry, sorry, *boning, getting busy*, you know, *knocking boots* or whatever, using her throat, using men, *using* men, or even being the mistress, being their flower, a flower, she's not being submissive, uh uh, no sir, she owns them, she owns them, they beg for her and that's who I most wanted to be like. And I've tried before to be like her, even though hers was a performance. (pause) You know I met that man in the street. (pause) Remember him? The man with the suit? He wore a hat and a suit, a really fine suit, he always seemed to be in some sort of a rush, his pace was quick (laugh), his suit moved around his body as he moved, he moved quick, quick, the material was expensive. (pause) I could tell by how the material moved around his joints, how it moved around his elbows and his knees. While he moved quick the material moved slow, and he moved between people real agile like while he carried a single banana in his left hand, gripping the single banana, and it left an impression on me, you know? What a thoughtful thing, I thought, him bringing sustenance to wherever he might be going next, a job interview, I thought, but he held no leather briefcase, no résumé, only the yellow banana, a fruit I never liked, too soft, too sweet, so then I thought he might be rushing to a person, a woman, or even a child, and later I thought maybe he just liked walking quick like that, sometimes too quickly, but I was hot on his heels. The skin on his heel was dry, it scratched my legs as he climbed over me—

I remember him now, I remember—

And for months we saw each other, months, weeks, in secret you know, and it was thrilling. (laugh) Always the smell of cut grass in the background. We wouldn't talk much, we didn't have time, but we had rhythm. Rhythm, we did. (pause) Like Ali when he rode the horse outside the Apollo with the black cowboys, remember, with the red-and-white checkered tie, and how the horse looked so small under Ali, and I looked small under the man with the banana, his shoulder with the stitches still healing, his stomach protruding like a soon-to-be mother, with his navel protruding, an outie, and two bags sitting under the closed eyelids, and when I rode him I touched the belly button and his top teeth would bite down on the bottom lip, the golden teeth and the wide bottom lip, wide, glossy with spit, nose flared, and the yellow always set against the purple of his left hand. He held the banana as we moved, and I didn't understand. I asked him, why? Why don't you let it go—

That's strange, it's a very peculiar thing—

Let go? He said it as if considering, but he wouldn't. He wouldn't. I didn't ask again. (pause) He ate popsicles whole. Someone was constantly cutting the grass outside the window, a window like this small one here. Once while he slept I tried to pry it from his hand, but, no, he wouldn't and I couldn't. I think he did release it when I wasn't in his company, though, because sometimes the banana was cold to the touch, cold as if it had been refrigerated. By the third month the fruit was too ripe, brown, black, inedible, cold and too soft.

YYYY

As Kendra's son climbs through the opening in the floor, he sees the woman. First her heels, her bruised ankles, her buttocks. The woman is standing in the corner of the room, facing the wall. Kendra's son is looking at her from this position, through the opening in the floor.

The woman's jeans are marked with blood. It's a small spot, a circle. Another person might not have noticed this mark, but Kendra's son does. In fact, Kendra's son takes pride in his ability to notice such things—small details and imperfections.

Perhaps they are the woman's favorite jeans, Kendra's son thinks, and this is why (despite her discovery on the previous evening of having bled through the folded toilet tissue, and the green panties, and then through her favorite jeans) the woman still chooses to wear them. The woman never articulated her level of commitment to these jeans, but it's entirely possible, Kendra's son continues to think, they might mean something to her.

Alice Coltrane playing the harp in the background while Kendra's son considers the muscles of the woman's uterus, contracting even now, even as he stands there looking at her, with his body emerging halfway through the opening in the floor. Yes, Kendra's son thinks, the lining of her uterus must be shedding.

And the woman does not complain about the pain. After all, they're only muscle contractions. She is used to it by now, she began her menstrual cycle early, at nine years old while lying on a twin bed at a religious summer camp.

At nine, the woman hadn't been frightened by the blood, as her mother had prepared her for all of that. The woman, who was then only a child, gathered the color on her small fingers, and she waited quietly for a camp counselor to stumble upon her impatient body.

Kendra's son is looking patiently at the woman in the corner. The woman is always in the corner.

It's not something to be misunderstood—the corners are where the woman resides. After many weeks of quarreling over the space, they came to this decision together. The woman comes alive in the corners.

It's not that the space is small. In fact, the room in which they're both standing—the woman in her corner facing the wall, and Kendra's son within his opening in the floor—is significant.

There's space enough for a very large bed, and a very large chest, and a large bookshelf filled with many books, a small sofa, a large built-in closet, and a very large handmade wooden desk, a lamp. But since they couldn't stop yelling and biting, they decided, very diplomatically, that the corners would be hers.

My favorite type of vision is the peripheral kind, the woman used to tell Kendra's son, *I like being on the periphery of things.*

Together they created a trap door in the center of the room, within the floor, so if Kendra's son were to enter he could avoid intruding upon the woman's corners.‡ Anytime Kendra's son

‡ Though they had not received the proper work permits for these Type-i and Type-ii alterations, and they had not filed their plans with the Department of Buildings or with the Landmarks Preservation Commission, and they had not hired a licensed master plumber or electrician, and they had not followed the Zoning Ordinances or complied with Zoning Law, nor any of the Building Codes, nor the Energy Conservation Construction Codes of the state.

sought entry from the door in the floor, he would already exist there, within the nucleus of the significant room.

And that's where Kendra's son stands, after having climbed up from beneath the house, through the tunnel in the earth. He's there, disheveled, but already in the center.

There are four separate doors for the woman, entrances and exits only accessible from the corners of the room. Two of them open onto a garden with rows of basil and rosemary and purple carrots and baby's breath.

So they each have their own means of entry and escape, and this, Kendra's son thinks often to himself, is the key to their harmonious affair.

They know how to share this space. There is no longer any ambiguity about which sections belong to the woman and which sections belong to Kendra's son. They no longer participate in quarrels of any kind.

In the night, they pretend to touch each other. From their designated and remote spaces they pretend to kiss, they pretend to whisper things. They reach out for each other's fingers.

The woman is undressing in the corner; she removes the bloody jeans.

The mark is momentarily hidden from view as she shifts the jeans over her backside, down her thighs, to her knees. She hesitates for a moment around the knees, and then the jeans are around her shins, calves, turning inside out around her ankles.

Finally, after some time, she is successful in their full removal, and the mark becomes visible from the inside, a dark burgundy speck. Then it disappears again as the material is crumpled and thrown, close to where Kendra's son stands, halfway through the opening of the floor.

The mark of blood is so close to Kendra's son.

The woman has a body she is not proud of, but Kendra's son thinks it's the best body he's ever had the pleasure to encounter, and he cannot help his erection.

The woman turns—her face is not the face you would expect for the body that accompanies it. But it is an interesting face, unexpected even, and Kendra's son enjoys it.

The woman fits her body neatly into the farthest corner, still standing, and brings her shoulders together. The woman stares up at the ceiling.

It's not a space someone would think to fill, the corner of a room, but Kendra's son can see how comfortable it might be. Whenever the woman fills one of the corners, he's startled by the corner's ability to gather a body—an embrace.

Kendra's son sometimes thinks he is missing out by having chosen the larger central space within the room, and he misses having the option of leaning against the corner, or touching the corner with the heel of his hand, or of placing his leather boots in the corner.

It seems the woman has not yet noticed his presence. In fact, Kendra's son has not found the courage to emerge fully from the opening in the floor. He looks at the woman from his crouched position, from this nucleus.

Kendra's son tries to stare at the same spot on the ceiling that the woman seems to be focused on, and they remain like this for some time. It is quiet moments like these that Kendra's son enjoys most of all, the stillness of them, and he reminds himself again of how lucky this arrangement is for them both.

Kendra's son is lost within his own thoughts.

If one looks carefully enough, Kendra's son thinks to himself, one might notice the shape created at the very point where the ceiling meets the adjoining walls of a corner—a shadow of the letter Y. Any room will display this upright letter at least four times, Y Y Y Y.

Kendra's son wonders if the woman notices this, if she is thinking of words that begin with the letter Y—*yard, yes, yank, yearning.* These four words aren't random associations for Kendra's son, he decided on them long ago, long before he and the woman segregated their living quarters. He named each corner back when he was nine years old. Kendra's son has always seen the upright Y Y Y Y and these words—*yard, yes, yank, yearning*—within any of the rooms he has inhabited. He has always noticed such things, small details and imperfections.

Kendra's son has never shared this observation with the woman, even though he thinks about it often, mostly at night. Kendra's son has kept this thought to himself.

The woman's eyes shine. She continues to stare at the ceiling from her place in the corner. The harp is playing and she's close to crying. When she begins to do so it is quiet, the liquid running to her upper lip, running to the corner of her lip, and despite Kendra's son's ability to notice such details, he does not notice this.

PENDERGRASS

Teddy, with his eyes closed, the widow's peak touching the center, three gold chains sitting against his chest cavity and the white tank top, the white teeth. Or with a cowboy hat, the fur, and always with the white suit, the white suit jacket, five gold chains sitting atop, the white pants, the full beard set against his full mouth, the sweat, the rasp, the screaming, wet, the heat from the stage lights, his long legs, legs set apart and twisting.

Teddy with his eyes closed in the green Rolls Royce Silver Spirit, young, the tree coming close and the malfunction, a sound from the neck, his legs set wide, for forty-five minutes a woman's perfume, and from the fifth and sixth vertebrae the light.

ADULT HEAD

And it's not what you believe it to be. It's blue, but also innumerably green. Innumerable, also yellow. Purple. Of course it's navy, black, cyan, royal and aqua, aquamarine, azure, baby blue, byzantine, celeste, cerulean, turquoise, denim, indigo, sapphire, but also teal, plus mint, kelly, olive, jade, army, artichoke—but colors can't describe a thing. More importantly, it's a mountain. It's a field in wind, or a mass, so big, pointy or rounded like laundry, warm like laundry, the sound's like an open hand to the cheek, or like broken glass, a pine cone crushing dry pasta, a splash/crash, sage. An adult head coming in and out of it, the largeness of the head against the innumerable hues, the shoulders, the neck praying. A crawl, a breaststroke, it hides and recovers the ear, the nostrils, the lips gathering and then holding breath, the eyelids closed, the hands like glass dropped from the counter, cutting completely into skin, or some other material, a lace curtain, and in the vastness of it there's this adult head, lapping up and down, in and out.

CABBAGE, THE HIGHEST ARCH

One head of cabbage, my grandmama says. She likes to tell me things. It is mostly about the people she despises, or about her mother. Sometimes it is about how to sauté the cabbage with bacon, green peppers, and onions. She tells me that she does not approve of a woman cooking only for herself, *it's selfish,* she says, *to cook only for oneself.* My grandmama drags her feet on the ground. When she is in motion everyone knows it, the neighbors know it, she makes a sound like sandpaper. We sometimes call her Sandy, to reference this sound.

Sandy has the smoothest skin, and on her feet the highest arch. Pieces of bacon and the cabbage in oil, in regular olive oil. Slices of onion, a whole onion, the big green pepper. My grandmama has her tight gray curls, and the white curls, the bridge of her nose, an expansive nose, her skin the most comprehensive brown, a dark brown, hairless, her sloped shoulders.

My grandmama tells me made-up things—how she once drew the attention of the Isley Brothers, Ernie or Chris, Rudolph, Vernon, O'Kelley Jr., Ronald or Marvin, how their hair looked soft, and their chest hair looked soft. How they walked down a spiral staircase with a taller man of no relation, and how he towered over them all, beautiful. She teaches me with her arms how to sauté all together: the cabbage, shredded and cut in half and then thirds, the edges cut off, in the big frying pan and on the stove, salt, the course salt, pepper, hot pepper at the end, in small batches, the cabbage sticking to the big pan, loosened with vegetable stock, or water.

THE MISCONDUCT OF SAND, AND THE SEVEN

Seven people once lived together in close proximity, and for a while this group did most everything together. Cooking rice-based meals together, collecting rare pieces of art, sweeping down the steps. It was a friendship devoid of jealousy or antagonism. It would last for seventeen years.

The bed was theirs equally, and the seven roommates slept together in it often. Sometimes, during the day, it would be three of them in bed, or the two of them, but usually it was the seven—fourteen ankles fighting the duvet. Fourteen bruised ankles.

The men slept close together and the women snored. The thighs of the men were exposed—people might have been surprised by the abundance of this exposure, but the women were not surprised.

There were three men and four women. Four of them were young, and three of them were old. One of the men was quiet but caused the most noise since he had decided to become a drummer. Six of them were lawyers. Seven of them did not believe in God. Two of the women were orderly, and two of them were untidy. Three of the men were orderly, and none of them were untidy.

The seven did not have much privacy.

While five slept, the two could not stop fucking. They climbed on top of the others, aligned themselves, kissed, slipped. Their heels fell against the protrusion of five collarbones. But the five never woke up, or stirred, and for the seventeen years they shared a home, none of them ever suspected that at one time or another the two could not stop fucking.

For the two it was not ideal or comfortable.

The community of seven lived in a home the color of a peach, with a yellow kitchen wall and wooden floors marked with burgundy dots. The large tree outside their home was infused with remnants of a bicycle—the *bicycle tree*, they called it. It bore no fruit, but the community of seven did not mind this; they were not afraid. They didn't believe the tree was cursed, in fact they leaned against it for shade and they touched the rusted bicycle with their fingernails.

As anxious children the seven had heard stories about this place and its previous inhabitants, and sometimes they would sit and discuss these stories as only anxious adults might—too loudly, too quickly:

> *The girl who lived in our home was sold into servitude to pay off the irresponsible purchase of an airplane, imagine! Her sister and mother and father sacrificing her for an airplane, and so for years she lived alone. And the white men who are now extinct trampled her elbows one day in the field, but a prince, a prince wearing a dirty ivory suit fell for her despite her missing elbows, and he tried hard to care for her. But the girl didn't feel fully content to be with him. Yes, yes, he was beautiful, with full lips and high cheekbones, his skin almost navy, but the prince was also a kleptomaniac, his soft hands could not stop the unauthorized collection of others' property, and the girl sometimes despised falling asleep next to him, in a bed that was too small for both of their bodies, and waking up with him, covered in the heaviness of his legs, the human chaos and warmth of heavy legs, and she*

sometimes also despised hanging up his ivory suits outside with wooden clothespins. The girl especially despised her job working for the white men who are now extinct, despised it so much that she would go to watch her bosses on her day off, every Tuesday, staring at them with contempt. And she could not forget that her family was gone, gone-gone, not gone as in dead, but in what she believed to be a voluntary exile, so eventually she abandoned the kleptomaniac prince too, to be consistent with the actions of her blood. He died alone in the kitchen, with all the objects he had stolen surrounding his body (golden earrings, chairs, quilts, and machetes), and the girl went to live on the Enflamed Mountain, which everyone knows will be gone soon, the wind is cutting it down, the entire mountain will be gone, gone-gone, it's erosion due to the wind and the change in the climate.

The community of seven did not wear suits. In fact they hated suits, perhaps because their grandparents had bequeathed them their own tarnished and hole-ridden dark blue, burgundy, ivory, gray three-piece suits. The grandparents had rigorously emphasized the importance of the suits and their washing, which was only to be done in the river. They had also provided their grandchildren with specific instructions on how to hang them up to dry, with wooden clothespins.

And so the seven refused to wear suits; they wore white dresses, blankets, and scarves—anything that would not confine them, anything that lacked buttons.

The seven agreed on mostly everything, but they could not agree on two things: 1) how they all met, and 2) who was the best looking.

Some thought they had met in the field, others thought they had met swimming in the river, the rest thought they had met near the *bicycle tree*.

They each found themself to be the best looking.

On the seventeenth anniversary of their friendship (which none of them realized was the anniversary as they disagreed on the circumstances of their first meeting), they bought a mirror. It was an oval mirror, and they hung it up against the yellow kitchen wall.

At first they enjoyed this reflective surface, how it echoed with accuracy and specificity their biggest flaws and most positive attributes; they even found beauty marks that the others had never pointed out.

The two who could not stop fucking would sometimes remove the mirror from its place on the yellow kitchen wall, while the others slept, in order to watch themselves climb on top, kiss, slip, and push their heels against the protrusion of five collarbones.

Unfortunately it wasn't long before things took a turn for the worse.

A few weeks after the purchase of the oval mirror, the seven began losing patience with one another: the three men became self-conscious (continuously covering their thighs), and three of the women stopped going to work at the law firm. The men who were once orderly became untidy, and the women who were once untidy became orderly. The men slept apart and the women could not sleep at all, and therefore did not snore. The two stopped fucking and began masturbating in separate corners of the house. One of them began praying to God, and all of them fell deeply in love with one another.

Jealousy came into their lives like an insect pressing against the glass.

And so it was inevitable that they would go their separate ways. One by one, the seven left the peach house, the yellow wall, the *bicycle tree*, the thin curtains, the smell of mud coming from the river.

They moved back into the homes of their grandparents. They began wearing the three-piece suits and other items held together by buttons.

They never shared a bed with so many people again, which they regretted deeply. The seven often murmured to themselves in their seven separate homes about the thing they missed most: it was the feeling of bruises forming around their ankles, purple, swollen, and unmistakable—on this they could not help but agree.

FORTY-SEVEN DAYS AGO

Five days ago, or twelve days ago, in the turquoise suit, he left. On the afternoon of June 8th, a man I knew left me for another. *She is kind*, he said. *The kindest person I've ever met. Thirty-three days ago* he told me, *V, I can't stay.* And I said, *Ok.* And he said, *I mean it, I have to go. Alone*, he added. He paused before he continued on, he could sense I was surprised. My hands moved across my knees, my eyebrows waited. He began chewing on the ice. He had on the suit, the turquoise suit, and it was ugly. I wondered if the kindest person had purchased it for him. It was not meant to be worn everyday, and yet he had, I realized, he had worn it every day. *Forty-seven days ago*, he abandoned me. It was June, humid. I was in the kitchen when he told me. Usually, after hearing his car in the driveway, I'd run down the steps and into the kitchen, jumping up onto the counter. It was a thing I always did, and he had always known to find me there. But on this day he was not himself. He pretended not to see me, even though I was directly in front of the entrance, sitting on the counter, and he was smiling, which was unlike him. My thighs widened against the limestone. I waited, my eyebrows waited. He went to get ice from the freezer, opened the freezer door, closed it, and then paused, as if distracted. Ice broke between his teeth, I heard the crunch, and then he turned, he saw me. Then, then he told me. *Ninety days ago* my husband left me. For weeks, months, I stayed in the kitchen, sleeping and defecating in his favorite room. I froze any liquid I could find: vegetable broth, apple cider vinegar, low sodium soy sauce, extra virgin olive oil, sesame oil, Worcestershire sauce, hot sauce, vanilla extract. That is to say I made ice from them, put them in the ice tray, and froze them. I chewed on the dark brown, beige, golden cubes. I heard the ice breaking between my teeth.

REAL NUMBER

In a fast food restaurant an employee standing behind a partition couldn't stop looking at my face and at my groin. He smiled at me. There were some people in line ahead, two of them were men, one of them was a woman, but the employee only looked at me and he asked for my number. Fifty-nine, I told him, and he said, jokingly, *but, but what's your other number, your real number?* He smiled, and his colleagues laughed, and the two men in line ahead of me laughed. I didn't laugh. The smell of peanut oil and chopped meat. The woman looked down at her feet. Someone else called my number then, *fiftyniiine,* the grease covered the paper bag, the grease covered it, and the employee couldn't stop.

SPALDING

When Jazmynn's partner left her, he left early, without much fuss. After he closed the door, slamming it, Jazmynn decided to gather all the items he had forgotten—the basketball, the cocoa butter, the cans of chicken soup, the cans of corn, the canned peas, the floral tablecloth, the rusted bicycle. She put the pile under the white sheets, on his side of the bed. Jazmynn napped with the objects; they all lay together.

Her partner had stared at her on the morning of his departure. They had been naked, his nails grazing her left breast. Her partner stared and his not quite straight teeth showed between his lips. He had a smile that made one wet, Jazmynn used to confide.

And he hadn't warned Jazmynn of his departure, he had simply begun packing his things—slowly, silently, one by one, into small rectangles. He was a good folder.

Jazmynn sat on the edge of the bed, back curved, stomach folded, chin resting on her knee, braid hanging against her spine. She was not surprised. She had known this was coming so she sat nearby as he folded, to show her acceptance of it, to show that she was granting permission.

Her partner's face was serious as he packed, full of tension. Jazmynn had wanted to laugh at this but decided against it. She sat there and watched him pack the rectangles and the spheres, the balls of socks—white, brown, black socks, purple socks—and the laundry detergent, the watch, the camera, the photograph of his friend Law, the razor, the eyeglasses.

Before his departure Jazmynn had helped him to shave his eyebrows, his back, his shins, and his arms with the razor. Together they rubbed cocoa butter all over his body. They shaved his pubic hair as an afterthought, the coarse curls sticking to Jazmynn's hands. He was dressed in his jeans, a white shirt.

When her partner was ready, Jazmynn was in the kitchen. She held the basketball in her hands: the weathered rubber and leather, the little orange bumps, the little light beige bumps, flattening. Jazmynn touched the engraved black indentation with her calloused fingertips: *Spalding*. Jazmynn bounced the ball lightly on the wooden table, the floral tablecloth sliding under its weight. It needed air, it didn't bounce with enthusiasm.

They had lived those eight years together in the same house, pale green, with a wraparound porch, big windows, 128 acres of land, their house set against it, the silver sky and the clouds, but they never learned to grow anything from it. They were too lazy to learn. They ate canned vegetables, canned chicken soup, canned corn, canned peas, dry pasta, canned tuna, and capers.

They spent their days washing the large windows, sweeping the dust from the bookshelf. Him—reading on the porch. Her—plucking the guitar. They would open their checks from Law, or they would sit on the kitchen floor with his picture between them.

They enjoyed not only the land but also its absence. They liked the large hole next to the house, muddy and emptied. A steamboat had been excavated from it. The steamboat had been lost in what was once a river. The discovery of it had been exhilarating, they were excited to have selected a fertile land.

On the last night they sat on the kitchen floor and waited for the rain to slow, they washed the windows, they ran the bath, they undressed and fucked and bathed with chamomile tea, green tea, they pretended it was a river, in the beige water they pretended to save people from drowning. On the last night he told Jazmynn about Law—about Law's skin, which was covered with eczema, and about Law's arms, which could lift substantial things, about Law's fingers, the way they pressed down on the keys of a piano, about Law's torso (too short) and Law's laugh (too loud and too high-pitched).

Law is jealous of you, he whispered. He touched Jazmynn's forehead as he whispered it. Jazmynn kept very still and calm as he spoke, but her face flushed.

On the last night they prepared for bed. Jazmynn's partner took a photograph of her while she braided her hair. Her fingers moved quickly between strands and when the flash went off she did not look away. She never saw the developed image, never witnessed the blurry hands.

The excavators who dug up the steamboat found things: 4,007 pairs of shoes, 751 pipes, 346 eyeglasses, 2,502 un-opened bottles of champagne. They didn't find any human bones.

They allowed Jazmynn and her partner to choose one object to keep for the trouble of having a large hole dug into their empty land. The rest would be stored in a white man's museum. Jazmynn chose the pipe. Her partner chose a bottle of champagne, but later changed his mind. He took the eyeglasses instead—*I want something I won't waste*, he told her.

The steamboat had been stuck in the mud, forty-five feet underground, waiting. Like Jazmynn, waiting.

He was gone. It was the third time Jazmynn had been alone in the house. She took out her braids alone and with her calloused fingertips. Jazmynn's undone, unraveled hair had waves in it, like water. She put on her red lipstick, her black panties, her black bra, her blue sundress.

Jazmynn took the key from its place on the highest shelf. She unlocked the front door (which had to be unlocked from the inside), because she didn't want her partner to have to knock. She waited for him to come.

Jazmynn made pasta with capers and tuna and olives. She sat on the kitchen floor with her back curved and in a pool of blue fabric. While she ate, Jazmynn read about steamboats and a river in a small book borrowed from the library.

The front door was opened as she read about the rerouting of the river, its change, its narrowing, why parts of what was once a river were now under homes such as theirs, under uncultivated land such as theirs. It was a slight creak, almost inaudible, but Jazmynn heard it and she knew with certainty that her partner would not be returning.

It was a woman who entered, a small woman, much smaller than Jazmynn. The small woman had brown eyes, the same black hair, only shorter, thicker, curlier, and she wore a large necklace, a vulgar piece. Jazmynn's hands held the plate of pasta while the small woman explained that Law had sent her to check on things. The small woman said, *Law sent me to check on things.*

The small woman closed the door behind her and stood there; she seemed anxious. After a few minutes of quiet Jazmynn decided to move, to go to the bedroom and grab the floral tablecloth and the orange sundress. She returned to set the table and serve the small woman a plate of pasta with tuna and olives and capers.

At Jazmynn's request the small woman undressed; she turned her back to do so. She put on the orange sundress (too long) and the red lipstick (too bright). The small woman ate ravenously.

After a few minutes of quiet, and of forks scraping plates, and of mouths chewing, the two women began to talk. They talked about different things: about what Jazmynn had learned of the steamboat—the metal and barnacles under the earth—and about the items that were found, the shoes and the eyeglasses, the pipes, the champagne.

They sat, a woman with a blue dress and a woman with an orange dress, talking like old friends.

When Jazmynn moved to the bedroom the small woman followed her. She brought the plate of pasta along and they continued discussing the importance of objects—how they tether us and how sometimes they help to create connections, but also how they can be meaningless garbage.

They undressed, they kissed.

Jazmynn told the small woman about her partner, about their second date, about how the maple syrup had stuck to their hands. The small woman already knew about all this, Law had told her. But the small woman had known nothing of the steamboat, nothing, and Jazmynn was relieved that her partner had kept something from Law. Jazmynn regretted having shared so much with the small woman, and in a separate retelling she altered the story of the steamboat altogether. They did not speak of it again.

The small woman shared only two things about herself:

that she had found the bulky necklace under a sequoia tree after her father had fallen ill, and that her father's name was John. Jazmynn never learned the small woman's name.

The two fell asleep on the bed with the basketball between them, and the rusted bicycle, the cans of chicken soup, the cans of corn, the canned peas, the floral tablecloth, and the plate of pasta the small woman hadn't finished. They fell asleep with the cocoa butter between them.

In the morning Jazmynn hoped that the small woman would be gone, but she wasn't, she was right there. The red lipstick was smudged on the pillowcases and the woman's face emerged from between the pillow and the rusted bicycle. Jazmynn took the small woman's hand and placed it on her left breast.

By the afternoon the two were washing the large windows together. It was in the middle of refilling the bucket with soapy water, and soaking the sponges, and gathering old newspapers that Jazmynn discovered the absence of the basketball.

She looked for it—in the hole, in the cornfield where the steamboat used to exist, under the kitchen table, under the floral tablecloth, on the highest shelf. Jazmynn cried. Into the pillows, into the cocoa butter, into the plate of hard cold pasta they hadn't yet thrown away.

The small woman cried, wailing. She pulled out her curly hair.

Jazmynn touched the woman's belly. It was hard and soft, terrible like a penis sometimes could be. Jazmynn moved her hand away when she felt it, as one might move away from a hot stove. But her calloused fingers could not help but reach. The index finger landed first, and she felt the s the p the a the l the d the ing humming underneath.

THERE'S D'ANGELO'S GAP

but it's also his bottom lip, his rotating bones, and how he seems taller, 5'6", but the torso seems longer, the yards of arched torso, the two front teeth like hard candy, a rope chain with a cross pendant, *Yahshua*, and his body hair: eight braids, straight back, between Stone's thighs eight braids, the eyelashes, the goatee, sideburns, underarm hair—Paul Hunter imploring him to sing like he's in the choir again, from his gut, in three takes, and at three he learned to play keys, hitting the closed fist against his chest, a black background hitting a nipple, the winged tattoo, how we forgot he wasn't mythical, throwing panties and not really listening, and how he hated all of that.

A DRY DROWNING, SPAGHETTI ALLE VONGOLE

place clams in a pan without water, a dry drowning, 1 kilogram for 4 people, wait until they open, but don't add salt,
clams still have the sea in them so take them out of their
shells, or keep them inside, if you want, throw them in the
hot pan with garlic, extra virgin olive oil, red pepper, parsley,
7 cherry tomatoes, and white wine, let the white wine evaporate, put a handful or 320 grams of pasta in boiling water,
place the pasta gently into the pan with the clams, stir together, add some pasta water, it's full of amido, full of starch,
it will create something, serve, eat immediately, otherwise it
should be thrown away

WET SAND USED AS AN ABRASIVE ELEMENT

The rumor spread. It was discussed so often that it became known. We couldn't help this; it's just something that happens when things are passed around. We ignored it. We drove to the orthodontist's office.

The orthodontist knew about the rumor. The orthodontist liked to hum and to whistle while he worked, and he did not look at us with any respect. The brackets were glued, one by one, and the wires pulled through like thread, and the double click. In the orthodontist's office a model airplane was set close to the instruments, for the purpose of distracting the siblings of his patients. The orthodontist had wanted to be a pilot. The receptionist knew about the rumor.

Afterwards, we went to the beach. Glory was at the beach. We sat with Glory; we spoke about the rumor with Glory. We showed Glory our braces. Glory already knew all about the rumor but allowed us to explain. Glory looked at us while we spoke. Glory didn't believe the rumor to be true, or wasn't concerned with it. When Glory spoke we didn't look at Glory, we looked at the sand or at our wrists. Glory's nose was running, but we didn't see, we weren't looking.

After we had finished discussing the rumor we were quiet. In the quiet we looked at Glory, her beautiful nose wiped clean, and at the mine trucks moving on the sand behind us.

The beach replenishment was in effect: yellow mine trucks, gigantic and filled with artificial sand. The workers like crumbs against the mine trucks. Mounds of artificial sand were being tossed around: 61,000 tons of sand, and the area becoming more and more vulnerable to erosion. This place was eroding; the beach was being replenished. The city had implemented the replenishment to remedy the damage, but it was already too late for all that.

Glory broke the silence—speaking about people we didn't know, about their knowledge of the land, things we couldn't grasp, evolutionary things, the harm of gossip, and about holes, extinction, about what is carried. We let Glory speak. We understood very little of what was explained, except when she spoke of Lloyd:

Lloyd met a man right here on this beach, this very beach, he met a man named D., D. he was known as back then, Lloyd explained, Glory said, *and the two had met because they had chosen spots very near one another on the sand, very close to the wet part of the sand and the water, a place not everyone preferred when setting their belongings down on a beach, people usually preferred the dry sand, and that D. had noticed, Lloyd said,* Glory said, *how both he and Lloyd began to chew on things around the same time—at 3:20 PM (chewing gum) and 3:23 PM (celery sticks) respectively—and they had sat for some time on this wet sand, chewing, before they both began to rub the wet sand onto their individual legs, or on their arms, and even underneath the soles of their feet, using the sand as an abrasive element, and when they realized this shared habit the men felt embarrassed or they felt something close to embarrassment. Lloyd went on,* Glory said, *that D. smiled and yelled, "I have eczema," and both their legs were covered with the wet sand, and soon after this,* Glory said, *they moved closer together. There were rumors about us for a long while, Lloyd said,* Glory said, *but after a while everyone moved on.*

And when Glory was done with this recounting we too used the fake sand as an abrasive element; we rubbed our legs and our arms. Glory didn't share anything else of substance, or if she did we were too distracted by the seagulls and the pretzels. With the wet sand on our palms we ate pretzels. Pieces of pretzel sticking to the metal wires around our gums, around the rubber bands, the artificial sand moving in and around our mouths. It was windy.

We swallowed the sand. Glory chewed the pretzels neatly. Glory played with the name chain around her neck. We removed our shorts; underneath we wore our lime-green bathing suits. The workers looked at our pubic hairs; the workers were like ants against the mining trucks. Glory remained dressed.

The younger workers seemed to know about the rumor, they looked at us. The older workers seemed not to know.

The birds were near, and when the name chain was broken it was because Glory had been chasing them off. Seagulls. While we sat, Glory ran around, she didn't care what anyone thought of her—not the young workers or the old workers, not anyone. The double-plated name chain was lost in this terrible sand. Imported sand. We used our feet as brooms. We dug with our nails. We dusted with our palms, but the name chain seemed to be buried and unreachable: *Glory*, 14-karat gold double-plated chain with the diamond-cut letters, the namesake letters and a heart design, lost.

We left Glory to search on her own. We left because we could not bear to see Glory in a state of despair; it wasn't the way we hoped to remember her. And anyway the workers were moving closer and closer, so we couldn't stay. We put on our shorts. We left her. We got in the car and we drove away.

The windows were open and as we drove off we could see Glory in the distance—with the yellow halo of mine trucks around her magnificent head, and the workers small as mice—before they were all out of sight.

When we came close to our neighborhood we heard someone yell the rumor. We didn't get a good look at them, but they sounded as if they might be young. Someone laughed and the young person laughed and the rumor was repeated, with less force, quieter, as the car was moving away from them; we were going home. And despite the heat we rolled the windows all the way up.

When we arrived and opened the car door the grass moved, and when we slammed the car door the grass moved, so even the grass seemed to know the rumor. The front door creaked; the steps creaked. We ran a bath. The water was loud as it rushed out; it knew. The artificial sand was everywhere, under our toenails and on the wooden steps, inside the mahogany china cabinet, in our eyebrows, on the purple painting, and on the banister, on the knowing banister.

We brushed the metal with a white electric toothbrush. Beneath the braces our teeth were stained. We flossed. In the bedroom we dressed, we turned on the lamp, we covered the lamp with a scarf and the white wall moved to lilac. Our hands washed in a lilac light; the lamp knew.

And the rumor grew. It became a myth, legend. Later, when the braces were removed, the teeth bleached and made straight, the rumor remained.

Then Glory left town. The orthodontist left town and the receptionist left.

The children wouldn't learn the rumor from us. They learned the rumor from their classmates.

It was passed around and passed down, handed around like an object. It was discussed in public and in private, in the post office and in the corner store, very close to the aisle with the Hot Fries. By this time the sand was gone, even its fake iteration, and the water was coming close.

Our children remembered the rumor even when they were no longer children. When they had our bodies burned and put into a single urn, or when they threw away all of our things and sold the car and all of the furniture (except for the mahogany china cabinet), they knew it. When they had to move inland, landlocked, they knew it. When the children had to get rid of even the last few possessions, when they walked down the street with the old mahogany china cabinet, the rumor followed them.[§] The children's teeth were naturally straight; no braces had been needed.

---

§   The reflection of the people across the street was in the mirror of the mahogany china cabinet—their open mouths, their open mouths multiplied, the swinging glass doors, mouths and our children's feet. In its interior the mahogany china cabinet held a mirror. The children who were no longer children's feet could be seen as they carried the cabinet to the junkyard (their faces couldn't be seen, or their legs or torsos). Their feet were harassed. The children carried the heavy thing and it was hard to carry, the beautiful mahogany and glass doors swung as they walked. The rumor had changed and the people across the street shouted this evolved rumor. The children pulled out the people's thin strands, oily, and sewed their lips shut with needle and thread. During the confrontation the mahogany china cabinet sat alone.

.

The earth folding in on itself, the water levels swelling irrevocably, and some form of the rumor persisting. Oh, how words persist! What the children's children felt in their bodies, in their left knee: a hurricane. We had left them nothing. Or with pollution there was nothing worth having. They had nothing except a knowledgeable precipitation—the hail breaking up the roof, and all the cracks in the building's foundation, in the earth's foundation, forest fires. In the eroded purple painting, in the trembling purple painting, the seismic waves persisted with an elastic and bouncing omniscience.

The children, the children's children's children, in their empty apartments, with their mouths and nostrils covered, with their oxygen tanks and the lack of materialism that surrounded them. There was nothing left to be said, there were no words to harm, but their bodies were prepared for words.

The children, the children's children's children no longer had to fear: the rumor was in their dry skin, in their hangnails, and in their low blood pressure.

Where there might have been a bookcase, the children's children's children stretched their bodies, they pulled their feet up behind them, their heels on their buttocks. Next to the space for the hat boxes the children's children's children's heads moved from one side to the other, and around the space for a deep freezer the children's children's children lunged. Their elbows held olecranon fractures and around the empty floors they lay themselves down. In their hazmat suits their chests touched their thighs and their toes gathered under, with their backs straight or rounded, the fingers of each hand almost touching, or touching the urn that held us, and held all the burned things, and because they were otherwise empty of heirlooms the earth cracked around them, and their knees were bent in pliés, grande pliés.

PEACH

When my mother dies, which will be very soon, I will buy myself a house. It will have large windows, and it will be mine. I will hang up photos of her on the walls, of when she was young. Young, like a peach. My mother has small breasts and full lips. The photos will show this. My breasts are larger and my hips are slighter. We're not similar in any way. I do not have my mother's long fingers, long toes, or the arches of her feet, her turnout, or anything else that belongs to her. I have nothing, nothing at all. When my mother dies, I will miss her like Fuller's Earth Powder, or a relevé, a jeté. I'll miss wiping down her body, and holding her discharge in my hands. My mother's brain is dying, and her hair. Her hair is brittle. Her hips are dying, the bones and her toenails dying, her earlobes, dying earlobes, and her knuckles, dying. Her bottom lip is drying and dying, her purple nipples are dead. I touch her back and feel the bump of her spine.

It is curved like a peach. Her skin is an accessory, hanging down from her buttocks like loose stockings, soft. My mother is light, she weighs nothing, and I carry her stupid body around for hours. Her hands move and it seems she can't control them. They move fast, fast, fast. She is happy, and then she is sad. She cries quietly. My mother is an alien, and the photos hanging on the wall of my new home will show this.

CEREMONY

The church was abandoned. They hadn't wanted to pay a venue or an institution, so they chose to have the ceremony in this place, a crumbling place. The entrance had no obstruction, no doors, and we walked right in. We sat in what remained of the wooden pews, three or four of them, most of us tightly squeezed in. The rest sat on the floor, on the ledges, on the altar. The windows were large and rounded at the top, windows shaped like healthy nail beds.

It wasn't a traditional ceremony; while the official delivered a sermon, people danced in the aisle. Or people did what they felt. Someone slept. A woman in a green skirt paced around, another spoke loudly on the telephone. A man, a relative of someone important enough, laughed and kicked his legs. There was joy, it seemed, joy in everyone's abandonment. Or relief in this abandoned place. We were gathered here against its intended purpose, and once a place is left or re-inhabited against its purpose the rules and regulations change. Another woman with long curved nails held a child; he snored softly against her bosom.

The people took the place over, made it something else.

It smelled of incense and sage and other dry leaves. There was a prayer, a speech. Next to me a woman's foot in a black heel. Someone had tears coming down their chin, a chin with a tattoo of a cross upon it, and another person lay on the floor with their arms out, as if forsaken. Someone rode on the pegs of a bicycle, performing something circular. Someone else flew a kite.

An older couple held hands; they wore black as if in mourning. In the pew they touched each other, laid themselves over each other. The woman behind the man, with her black dress lifted up and her underwear exposed (also black). The man's beard came down to his clavicle and his feet were exposed and dry. The woman's piercings ran around the highest part of her nose. The man had no control over what she chose to do with him. His church shoes (also black) were sitting near him. She entered him. Her church hat (also black) moved behind her neck and she didn't reach for it, she let the head covering go, her locs exposed to the apostle, Paul.

In the background an organ played something.

Instead of wafers, slices of blood orange were passed around. It was an unusual choice; I had never eaten fruit inside a place of worship. People had the red of the orange on their fingertips; they wiped the juice on their clothing: onto their silk chiffon, onto their lace, onto their cotton. Someone had a rosary wrapped around their wrist and they moved it up and down, the beads rolling.

When someone decided to speak from the altar there was no one to contradict them, anyone could step up and lead if they wanted. The echo of these new voices was deafening, unnatural, the space too big to hold it. These leaders said things we didn't understand, private things about those at the center of the ceremony, details that didn't seem appropriate to share. Someone else (not a leader) sang *make it last forever*. On the floor beside me there were reading glasses, a veil, a book of hymns, the seeds of a blood orange.

There was no electricity and when night came the church was dark. Someone tossed flowers around. We stayed put. We lit candles (not church candles but scented candles: apple, rose, beach dream, salty waves, and lavender petal). More food was being passed around, and everyone ate it without asking questions. All the food was circular, spherical or cut into circular shapes. It tasted of sage, cinnamon, game, and scotch bonnet. A honey biscuit from Church's Chicken, hard-boiled eggs. There was a dessert made with lavender, honey, coconut milk, rice, banana leaves, fig.

In the candlelight I could see an individual passing very close to my face, exposing their belly button. It wasn't the belly button but the lips that caught my attention, the lips were brown, and where the lips met, in that interior layer there was pink, two-toned lips. The belly button was forgotten in light of the brown and pink lip.

On my right a pregnant belly was tightly bound in a bronze strapless dress.

Tea came around, chamomile or green, there was a choice. Someone yelled the choices out loud: *green! chamomile!* I chose chamomile because I wanted to rest. And I did, for a while. When I awoke I had been moved from the pew to the tiled floor. The tile was intricate, a mosaic tile made by hand—burgundy, white, blue, green, cold. The church bells that had once been suspended were also on the mosaic tile floor, rusted. They sat near my neglected body, near my nose. The bells were large, unnaturally so, and they held markings, illegible scrawling and dates. The bells weren't in use; they were quiet.

From the floor I could see that the walls were pink, an odd color for a holy place. The plaster was peeling, the paint peeling, and the pink mixed with yellow, brick, green, with mold. Some of the windows were broken and the cool air came in. The beams on the vaulted ceiling were untethered; pieces fell on our heads.

Behind the altar a wall was missing. Or I should say it had been removed, or erupted, demolished. The structure of the church became fragile when viewed through this missing barrier. A leader singing on the altar had her back to the opening, she wore a clerical robe and when the wind moved it around we could not take her seriously. The cemetery could be seen behind the woman with the flapping robe—mausoleums, tombs, inscriptions, and the thousands spent to bury, right in front of us, money in the ground.

A bottle of wine rolled on the floor. Pigeons flew around, or walked. They shit on us. They hung around, walking in pairs. We were growing tired and it was loud. Young people spray-painted the silhouette of a man in burgundy, yellow, greens, he had no discernible features. No face. In the farthest corner the statue of a camel lay on its side, not seeming to belong but unmovable. The children rode the camel.

The things I had brought along with me for the ceremony very quickly proved to be inadequate: a tinted lip gloss, a greeting card with money folded inside and my initials signed at the bottom (R.I.), a reusable water bottle, sanitary napkins, nose tissues, reading glasses, my driver's license and cellphone, mascara, a flower, seashells, a pack of mints.

There were mosquitoes everywhere. I scratched my legs.

The ceremony continued without interruption. Children played games in the corners; their parents didn't pay attention. They pushed each other in the back, they took off their collared shirts and their stockings, their hair barrettes, they splashed in puddles of holy water, they pretended to baptize each other, soaking their hair in it. A grasshopper moved from my elbow to my forearm to my middle finger.

Around us there was an accumulation of objects: wallet-sized photographs, hats, loose coins, a pocket mirror. I couldn't orient myself to this space, so I stood up.

The walls were more fuchsia than pink. We waited for

something more to happen, but nothing did. A bar of spirits lined the fuchsia wall—bottles of all sizes and shapes, dark and clear, white and creamy, blue. Near my feet a train map and dry eucalyptus leaves. We tried to be patient. Even the children tried, but when the first person began to complain it affected everyone, and then everyone felt free to complain, even the children. Someone took the milky alcohol bottle and drank from it.

Later we were reprimanded. Then we were let out, so we gave it up, we left.

When we arrived for the second day of the ceremony everyone seemed tired. Most had dark circles around their eyes. No one wore their best; we wore what was available to us. We hadn't expected a second day, we'd believed the ceremony would follow the traditional timeline, but we had been mistaken, the leaders expected our attendance.

The second ceremony was not in the church, it was in a park, though the air was too cool for it. When it began there was nothing different about it; it was the same. The speeches and the songs were the same, the people were the same, the blood oranges and the food we could now identify: goat, rice and peas. A dessert we could see but did not know: fig, banana leaves, rice, coconut milk, honey, lavender.

The children played in the corner of the park behind the trees. A sermon, an exposed abdomen. It was the same. There was recognition on the faces, we were to experience this again and we were to enjoy it.

I tried to show enthusiasm.

The second ceremony was almost over. I knew it because it was the same thing. The things were carried; we got up to go. Once again we were reprimanded, like we knew we would be, we were stopped. Then something new—we were led to a fast food restaurant.

The smell of fried things was strong. The fluorescent lighting didn't flatter us. We sat or stood where we could. Most stood. We weren't hungry for this food, we had already eaten so much of the rice dessert and of the goat, but we ordered. One by one we stood in line, we received an order number, and we picked up our food from the counter. We collected the condiments, the straws, the utensils, and the napkins. We sat or stood to eat, we burped, and we didn't speak a word.

FALSE LASHES

It's hard to know where to begin. The bed was clean, and I liked that. The sheets were white; the pillowcases were white. The floors were wooden; there were twenty and thirty-five pound weights in the corner. A soy candle and a vase with dried flowers, a painting of a face on the wall. We sat on the white bed. It was a queen-sized bed, not a king. It felt firm and we sat close enough to touch. We didn't touch.

We sat there at first. He talked a little. I had come to fuck; it was the only reason I had come. I didn't want to talk, especially not about the extinction of any species, of a black rhinoceros. When I touched his hand I think he understood something.

And when we were done he touched himself and talked a little more. When we were done we were on the floor. I wanted to go but listened. And then I couldn't listen and instead began to recall the way he'd bit me. The way I'd spread him, the way it felt before we penetrated, the goosebumps on his skin, the whole of his body.

The focus of the encounter had been the hands, the nail beds, the individual fingers, the veins on the top, the lines in the palms, the knuckles, the hangnails, the tissue and ligaments of the hand. I rode his hands and I forced them out, into my mouth and out of my belly button. I ate his hands, I wrapped them around my clavicle and around my right hip. The thighs enveloping the hands. His fingers were wrapped around my toes, on my shin, and inside my meniscus.

People believe the lips to be essential, and they are, but it's the hands that know everything and find everything and are most capable. The hands are braver or looser. The fact that his right hand became broken was an accident; things had gotten away from us. So it was only one hand that continued its pursuit; we were left with one hand. And this lone extremity did its job. It scratched, it began, it climbed, it unfastened.

The broken hand was done, limp, but the other was tickling. It was moving around the scalp, massaging and tapping. It was under the breasts and right around the nipple.

It lifted the nipples out of the way, it moved the membrane and it entered simultaneously, it caressed. The hand dipped, it curved, and sometimes it retreated.

My lip liner was smudged on the working hand, and the broken hand was clean. The active hand pulled on my piercings. The hand was glistening, flicking. It was soft, or it pushed in a soft way, it spun. It peeled off my false lashes one at a time; it touched the bridge of my nose. The other hand was limp, but this one went back to my hips, it supported my hips. It waded in my material. It ruffled the solid and held it in its grasp, and the hair on the nape of the neck, which was cut short enough and neat.

The hand brought the eyes along with it, the eyes, imagine it. Wherever the eyes went the hands went too. With the eyes it pointed and held on, it decided something. With the eyes it didn't play. It spun. With the eyes the hand hesitated.

The hand, it also let the eyes rest, the eyes were closed and the mouth was opened. Wide, the hand was using two fingers, three, and the other hand was broken. It sometimes grabbed my own hand and brought them both together to the stomach. It felt like snow. In the cognizant hand, the viable hand, a spliff appeared and the smoke rose up. The rings on the hand fell off and a cherry Blow Pop appeared between the thumb and the index. The hand helped to distribute the gum in its center.

The hand held a comb and raked it through all the body hair available: the pubic and the underarm, the eyebrow, false and real eyelashes, the hair on the buttocks, the leg hair, the back hair, the toe hair, the upper lip, the hair between the brows, the head of course. Everything was combed and laid down.

The hand moved and its wrist held three large scrunchies. The knuckles held my chin up and my cheek. The hand picked up the twenty and thirty-five pound weights, it curled them; the hand curled around my knees and brought me up. Then we were down again, up and down in a matter of seconds.

The fingers separated, they did their own things. They moved not in harmony or in accord or in congruence with the others or in coherence or in coordination with anything, they moved in discord. The thumb, it wanted something different than the index finger, which only wanted one thing. The middle finger wanted nothing and opted out. The ring finger was the most enthusiastic, and the pinky. They parted things.

And when the mouth arrived at the breast the hand cupped around it.

And when the mouth arrived at the breast the hands (both hands, the broken and the unbroken) were performing surgery.

And when the mouth arrived at the breast, the hand hid. The hand pulled the bubble gum out, stretched it long, wrapping it the length of the body. The broken hand joined in, they moisturized everything.

And when the mouth arrived at the breast the hands were gone from me. They focused on the self, on himself. They touched their own body, what had always been familiar and neat. They knew things about that body. The hands wanted me to go. They snapped, they made sounds, they clapped, they made a song. They removed the earring backs; they took the tiny earrings out of the lobe. For a while they rubbed. They were intertwined. They lost themselves and then they found things. The eyes stayed closed. The hands went on. I got dressed. They sank and I was up.

THE NEW HUSBAND

Hominy is a woman of a certain age. Hominy can no longer perform many of the movements that young people take for granted, but she's not yet old either; she can still fuck.

Hominy is remarried. Hominy has moved in with her new husband. She sometimes enjoys the company of this man—when they are sleeping, or sitting in silence—but mostly she feels disrupted by his presence.

To alleviate this feeling, Hominy sends her new husband out into the street unexpectedly, interrupting him in the midst of eating or bathing, pushing his still wet body along the corridor and down the steps, and slamming the door against his back. Without complaint, her new husband stands outside their home wrapped in a towel, waiting for however long he must.

Hominy did not feel this way when they began their courtship.

In the beginning, she was attracted to this man. He was charming. He wore his hair in braids, all of them attached to his scalp, and she liked seeing the spaces between, the exposure of the scalp. His voice was loud. She enjoyed this too. In the beginning, they would stay up late, trying to push the limits of their time together—3:15 AM, 4:21 AM, 5:09 AM. Like teenagers. His mouth always moving toward her.

She would record the precise times of these early interactions, writing the hours and minutes into a blue gridded notebook. In the midst of this record keeping, this new man who would soon become her new husband would whisper the strangest things into Hominy's waiting neck. Phrases that would force her to pause, to drop the pencil on her thighs, to laugh, mouth wide, bottom teeth exposed. Hominy would push his body away from her collarbone to begin her task anew: looking down at her left wrist, picking up the pencil from her exposed thighs, neatly writing down the hours, the minutes.

In the time since their civil ceremony, Hominy has stopped writing the details of their interactions. In the time since, her new husband has begun to frown. Not in a subtle way, but very deliberately. Frowning in the morning and in the afternoon. Often, he waits until Hominy looks up from her book or until she turns away from the sink where she's been washing the wine glasses. As she moves toward him, catching his eye, there it appears, a frown.

His hair is no longer twisted together. His scalp is concealed and his hair is cut short, gray and uniform. In the time since, the new husband has begun to hide his hands. He wears plastic gloves to avoid germs and also to maintain their suppleness. He does not touch Hominy anymore without the cover of latex.

The new husband only removes the gloves to shower or to caress Hominy's hair while she performs fellatio. Only then does he remove the right glove and the left, pressing his fingertips into her graying twists. His ungloved hand, the right hand, moves slowly through, flakes floating down onto the wooden floor and onto her brown shoulders. Hominy suffers from a dry scalp. Hominy's new husband watches her tongue move, and on his most beautiful lips: a frown.

The home Hominy shares with the new husband is messy, objects and junk having accumulated. From her spot on the couch Hominy can see cleaning products, some clothing, a dark sock, and to the left: five stacked books, makeup brushes, lotion, a damp towel, the open window.

Hominy can hear people moving, the street sounds from outside. Yelling. The home she shares is small. If she turns her head to the right[*] there is a kitchen—the corner of the sink with the greens already soaking, the counter, the dirty pots on the counter, and nearby an unopened box of biscuit mix, one sack of lentils, lemons, four sweet potatoes, ears of corn, two beets, a knife lying flat on its side, capers, anchovy paste, the reading glasses sitting out of their case. If Hominy turns her head to the left[**] there is a bathroom: the tub half-filled with water, cold water, two soft-bristled toothbrushes, floss, soap, and a bundle of oranges, twenty-seven oranges, spread around the base of the toilet. In the living room the guitar case stands in the sun, the roses are wilted and dark purple, the lemon water has cooled.

The new husband often leaves without saying where he might be off to. During the times she's left alone, Hominy explores their home. She finds items that do not belong, left behind by others. Hominy pretends that she owns these objects in order to avoid acknowledging their potential owners: she wears the old retainer, uses the unused tampons,

---

[*]   which Hominy refuses to do in this moment of narration

[**]   which Hominy refuses to do in this moment of narration

expired multivitamins, the last remnants of toothpaste, thong underwear, and she wears the blue-red-pink-black scarves over her thinning hairs.

Hominy drives the car only when she's alone, never with the new husband. On her days off, when she's left to her own devices, the warm car delights her. The sun is hot on her legs when she releases the clutch or when shifting gears. Moving to neutral, stopping at a red light, moving down to first. Releasing the clutch, foot on the gas. She drives to places the new husband doesn't approve of. When she's alone Hominy doesn't have to wait to consume things; she lets fried foods swell her belly. When she's alone Hominy's dehydrated. In the car, she looks for distractions. In the car, Hominy masturbates.

When it's humid, Hominy sits and waits for the rain. Hominy is humid and waiting or she's falling asleep with her legs set apart, and she wakes up with her sweater sticking to her back. She wakes up with strange men looking into the driver's side window, their noses pressed against the glass. In the car, Hominy smokes weed.

Hominy goes to the market high as a kite; she buys three bananas, two lemons, tomatoes, plantain chips, facemasks, a bag of potatoes, a head of cauliflower, coconut pancake batter, coconut yogurt, coconut extract, coconut milk, and coconut water. Hominy's skin smells like her sister's, like flowers.

When the new husband is on his way home, Hominy turns the car around. She drives back. She parks the car in the street, but she doesn't park well. She locks the car doors. She enters the apartment. When the new husband returns, he touches her shoulder with his wrists.

Hominy learned things when they began living together: **number one**: that the new husband makes noises in his sleep, a kind of humming. When he makes these noises in his sleep, she digs her nails into his arms to interrupt. Hominy dislikes the new husband dreaming of things she cannot know, and she dislikes that there exists a musicality within him, so she digs her nails into him, **number two**: that the new husband prefers for Hominy to whisper, **number three**: that the new husband doesn't like to be stared at for longer than a few seconds, four or five seconds, **number four**: that the new husband likes to sleep with his face near Hominy's legs, exhaling onto her legs, inhaling near her legs, and that he doesn't like sitting with his legs set apart, he disapproves of Hominy's legs, set apart, **five**: that the new husband likes to smell things before he consumes them: peanut butter, fish soup, baking soda, ackee, pistachio shells, labia, turmeric, **number six**: that the new husband clips his nails in the corner of the bedroom, on the wooden floor. The grayish white lunula—moon-like pieces—he cuts them, the new husband, he sits on the floor for hours with the tools: the emery board, clippers, the orange stick, the cuticle trimmer, the buffer, his back dangerously curved.

The apartment belongs to the new husband. It doesn't fit Hominy, but she places her things in it. She places her things next to the items that do not belong to her, her few items of clothing: a mint-green sweater and a leather jacket lined with wool. A first-edition Fran Ross, a spider plant.

When they eat together they use one fork, or one spoon. Sometimes they use a knife. Hominy and the new husband feed each other, taking turns with the singular utensil, sitting close together. They starve, waiting for the other to return home. They sometimes wait for hours, weak and waiting with the solitary instrument in hand.

Other things Hominy and the new husband share: their obsession with leaving things about. Hominy and the new husband like to clean *around* objects, dusting only the places they choose. A selective dusting. They also share a love of opening the windows wide, no matter the season. Also, the delight at sleeping in and of watching documentaries late at night: they watch *No Maps on My Taps*, the Harlem men loosen their ankles, they swing their arms, they click, they perform with earth-toned suits, browns.

Hominy and the new husband enjoy painting their fingernails with the blue, the green, and the clear nail polish. They share the polish. They like the smell of acetone. Sometimes they spill it on the wooden floors and they don't clean it up, they don't lament the stains.

Hominy wants a child with the new husband. Sometimes she thinks of this boy, of how she would prepare him for things. Even at this late age, Hominy hopes to have a boy.

When Hominy becomes pregnant, she finds the new husband does not share her desire. A pill is procured, swallowed, and that is that.

There is a kind of violence when the new husband calls Hominy a stupid fucking bitch. The next day they laugh, they fold warm clothes, they watch the *Tip Drill* video on repeat, Whyte Chocolate moving and the credit card sliding; they sleep with their legs intertwined.

When the new husband doesn't return home for the night, Hominy sleeps with both windows open. Fireworks rattle, loud, and she dreams of a woman's inner thigh, of a woman's stockings inside her mouth. For the most part Hominy sleeps through the night. Unless she consumes a large piece of watermelon, sweet, metallic. The large watermelon wakes her up and Hominy hits her elbow on the bathroom door. Hominy moves in the dark to the toilet. Twice, three times, five. This natural diuretic, the pink pink watermelon always wakes her.

Hominy and the new husband go for walks. They walk around their neighborhood at night. It's not a quiet neighborhood. They see eight or nine people in the street. Numbers ten and eleven are indoors, standing together in their dining room. The interior of their home is lit up bright. This pair has chosen not to purchase blinds, not the wooden ones, nor the hard plastic ones, not curtains. They watch them, they see their plain white furniture.

When Hominy and the new husband don't walk, they

sit on the rooftop. It's not quiet. The birds are yelling and the slanted tiles are hot under them. Hominy doesn't wear a bra; her breasts are low and free. When she's up on the roof, Hominy can see the birds and the trees as they move. With each movement the trees say, *your body is an afterthought to him, you shouldn't have come.* Hominy ignores the angiosperms.

When Hominy waits for the new husband to come home she is restless. She moves from the queen-sized bed. Her eyes are open, her body is up, her back is rounded, Hominy throws the covers aside, her joints ache. When she waits she wears a gown unfit for sleeping, delicate, a bright color, sheer, long, full, her nipples visible. Hominy wears no makeup; she's unmade and waiting.

Hominy is waiting for him to come, but he will not. Not tonight or the next night. When she's waiting for the new husband (which is all the time), Hominy moves about aimlessly, pretends to look for her cellphone, pretends to find it. She picks it up. The battery is down to seventy-nine percent. In case the downstairs neighbors are listening, Hominy pretends to call someone. She pretends to have someone to call.

She pretends to hang up. Hominy moves slowly, not picking up her feet, bare feet sliding from here to there, a sound like sandpaper.

When Hominy is waiting for the new husband she walks to the living room, which is also the bedroom. Past the convertible couch/bed, past the television, and then she passes a framed photograph, a dying plant, many piles of books. The room is rectangular. The ceilings are high. Hominy moves toward the kitchen, then changes her mind, turns back toward the living area. She sits on the radiator. The couch/bed is visible from her position, unmade, and the floor is like a sea of discarded clothing.

Then she decides; Hominy moves definitively to the kitchen, ten steps away from the couch/bed. She counts the steps. She thinks of Toni Braxton, her low register and her mumbling. She looks at the corner where the ceiling meets the adjoining walls. She looks at the windows, at her hands, and down at her long ashy legs.

When she's waiting, Hominy grabs the knife. She sits at the kitchen table. She cuts and deseeds twenty-four green chilies. Inevitably she touches her nose, her upper lips. She rushes to pour milk into a bowl, to dip her face into a bowl of milk. Her hands burn; her fingertips burn. Hominy is submerged in milk.

Hominy and the new husband begin to sound alike, to smell alike. They begin to sweat from the same areas: under their arms, from the bridge of their noses, down their lower backs. They wear the same deodorant, the same lotion, the same perfume, conditioner, shampoo, and the same hair oil. His beard smells of her scalp, and her scalp smells of his pubic hair. Their penmanship becomes identical—Hominy's miniscule writing meshed with the new husband's leaning letters. They borrow things from each other. They sign each other's checks. They use the same vocabulary: *fuck that, folks, unbelievable, true, pigs, good riddance.* Hominy can no longer remember to whom the words belonged in the first place.

Hominy takes the whispering from the new husband. He prefers it. Even when she's alone in the house, even when the customer service representatives plead with her to do so, Hominy does not raise her voice above a whisper: *Ma'am,* the customer service representatives say, *please, please use your diaphragm to provide your card information.*

For Hominy and the new husband, there isn't always much to say. There are days of utter silence. There are days when Hominy cuts a yellow fruit in bed and the juice collects under her oval nails, and the new husband sits in the kitchen turning the pages of the newspaper with his gloved hands. Those days they don't speak at all. Other days the couch/bed is filled with sand. Hominy and the new husband came from the beach, they fucked on the beach, with people around them they had sex in the sand and then they brought it home with them. Sometimes Hominy and the new husband sleep through the night like children.

They play dominos, and Hominy likes to watch the way his hands shift the pieces around.

When the new husband returns he doesn't say hello to Hominy, not when he opens the front door, and not when he goes into the bathroom. Not when he shaves his chest, or when he bathes, or when he uses a towel to dry underneath his arms, not when he steps over twenty-seven oranges and not when Hominy strips down to nothing.

PASTA, FAGIOLI + COZZE

The mussels are forced open, or they are made to open. With an instrument or with fingers they are cleaned, they are knocked together, they are rinsed. The black and brown and purple mollusks are thrown in the pan, they move around like rocks, the knob is turned to the right, clicking, and the fire heats underneath, the mussels are covered with a copper lid and some of them are stubborn, the ones that refuse are discarded, but the ones that open are discarded too, some of them, for their smell and for other unsatisfactory details, they will be tossed into plastic, the suitable ones are left to cool. And the shells are emptied, the orange cores are set aside, the sea water is set aside. In the meantime the cannellini beans are sautéed, in a tall pot the garlic cloves, the olive oil, parsley, red pepper, maybe an onion, maybe celery or pancetta (though I put neither) and not a carrot, never a carrot, and the hot water standing by, but it shouldn't be abused, the fagioli should not be made too watery, and when the boil sets in the pasta is stirred in,[††] always for less than the allotted time, and when it's all over the mussels are folded in with a flick of raw oil, more parsley, but the carrots, the carrots no.

[††] Preferably tubetti, tubettini, broken spaghetti, or a mixture with similar cooking times, or even a pacchero.

540i

Droplets pull and push against the glass, moving in every direction. The air is blowing on the glass and then the water is rushing. A piece of light plays against the windshield, forming shadows on the dashboard, the seat, and on Bruna's dry hands.[‡‡]

The water is rushing, rushing out against the green car, a 2003 BMW 540i. This artificial typhoon is summoned, loud against the metal. Bruna is reminded of a baptism. The vehicle is submerged. She thinks of holy words: *thou, doubt, shall, unto, save, whole, thee, obey.*

Bruna's mouth is open and the phlegm is resting in her chest. Bruna is often sick, coughing, or otherwise scratching her throat. So that's how she is in the car wash: nose

---

‡‡ Bruna's hands make her seem older than she is. In fact, Bruna is definitively young. Someone broke up with her because of the look of her dry hands. She places her dry hands on the steering wheel. Bruna refuses to hide them, she refuses to be ashamed.

stuffed, sitting, scratching her throat. In front of her: a Volvo, a Nissan, an Alfa Romeo. Bruna touches the orange sweater around her neck. She's sick. Or she's been crying and her nose is stuffed. Her lips are dry and her tongue is dry from this breathing through her mouth. She can't smell the leather seats or the tree-shaped air freshener swinging in her peripheral.

It's nighttime. Bruna watches the road from the reflection in the rearview mirror—blurry people on their way to work, or to the fish section of the supermarket. Behind the Nissan, the Volvo, the Alfa Romeo, and the 540i there's the sound of a motorcycle rushing past them, past the car wash on Boston Road. They inch forward, the fluorescent lighting in their eyes. They lift the beige visors, folding them in place. They shut off their radios. They listen to the whistling of the phlegm in Bruna's chest, the air behind her teeth as she breathes, and the tracks that are moving the sixteen tires forward.

The soap falls. Despite having been raised in it, Bruna no longer remembers how religious words fit together—*in the name of the Eucharist, all glory is yours*—she can't remember, not any of the verses of the catechism, or how the voices of the Corinthians might sound. Ashes were placed upon her forehead as an adolescent, and she knows the pressure of a priest's finger on her skin, the ashes falling onto her nose, the pipes of the organ, the dark mark small and illegible.

The 540i is pulled farther into the tunnel. The track underneath is clunking, clunking. Bruna watches the soap moving on the windshield, moving like unsalted butter in a nonstick pan. Moving down. In semicircles. Up.

It's quite beautiful. If someone were in the 540i with her she would tell them. She would pause and tilt her head to the right, breathe in, sigh, breathe out through the mouth (as her nose is unwilling to open for air). If someone were with her she would want them to notice this tilt of her head. She might offer it discreetly: *It is quite beautiful?*

Bruna is alone.

Except for the car wash attendant, Bruna's alone. The other cars are gone: Nissan, Volvo, Alfa Romeo. She's the last and it's late. Earlier, hours before, when she'd handed the car wash attendant the discounted fee, he chose not to meet her eyes.

Droplets of soap continue their swimming; under the fluorescent lighting it's reminiscent of the moment after sex, when the fluid drips down Bruna's thighs, dripping, smelling of hydrogen peroxide. Or when it lands outside of her purple nipples. Her purple nipples are sore and swollen as she sits in the 540i, as they usually are during this time of the month. She is menstruating, and the smell in the car wash tunnel is unmistakable—hydrogen peroxide.

She thinks of her mother and of the name she decided to give: Bruna, Bruna, *Bruuuna*. As a child Bruna heard it being yelled in frustration. Her mother didn't like the name, it was a name chosen to encompass her strong distaste for this child, a child who looked only like the father.

Bruna means *dark-haired, dark*. The name reduces her to her most obvious quality. Bruna was born with a dark mane of hair. She sometimes calls herself Una. Or Runa. Or Brun. Bru. Br. Na. Run.

In the 540i, Run's hair is no longer dark. It was dyed yellow, with a bottle of bleach and peroxide it was dyed.

Yellow is the complementary color of purple, Run thinks, and so she's delighted that her hair complements her sore purple nipples. As a habit, Run will sometimes touch her nipples while watching television in her bedroom.

Bruna's yellow hair is stuffed in the mouth of her orange

sweater. This creates the impression of short hair, the length being something she can reveal or suppress as she chooses, the artificial yellow.

Van Gogh used an abundance of yellow and purple in his paintings. Run likes *The Bedroom* with its violet walls and yellow chairs, and so she sometimes calls herself Van.

Van chooses not to show the length of her yellow hair to the car wash attendant. His hair is dark.

The mitter curtains approach, swaying and swinging like the drunk. Then they are upon her and up on the windshield of the 540i. With a loud thump, the curtains cover and uncover the glass, darkness and light alternating, the curtains standing, lying down, standing, hesitating, lying down again, heavy and indecisive on the windshield.

Van wonders what the car wash attendant thinks of this car washing technology, if he finds his job ridiculous, if he considers it unskillful when he prepares for work in the morning. If so, Van doesn't agree with his impatience, she believes the job is functional.

Van has been conditioned to be complimentary and to *sit still, for God's sake*, which is how Van sits now in the 540i, knees touching, ankles crossed, head leaning.

The car is pulled forward and Van shifts in her seat. There is discomfort in having been conditioned to sit so still, for the sake of God. Some sound startles her and now her knees are apart—a harlot's gap.

The soap and water drip down like holy water.

Rain sometimes contains hydrogen peroxide, Van's male boss once told her. *The dripping is like seminal fluid, or the first milk, colostrum, which contains peroxide too.* In the small office kitchen her male boss had whispered in her ear, *colostrum helps the immune system of babies.*

The chemicals, the foam, disinfectant, air and water, hydrogen, the spermatozoa, the weak immune system of newborns, oxygen, and the long strips of cloth moving all of these things around.

The 540i, forest green, continues forward. Van's head leaning back, she watches the car wash attendant in the rearview mirror.

There is soap and then it's gone, the water returns, hitting the car, pounding the car with air, drying, and then the dirt. She has paid $1 extra for this dirt service. She's paid a total of $6.

The dirt comes from the car wash attendant: mud and

sand, grease and oil. He throws buckets of it on the windshield. It's on the glass, on the windshield wipers, the green car. Van thinks of abandonment, of a man who left her only for the look of her hands, not for another woman, as her family had first believed, but to live the life he felt he deserved.

Van thinks of hourly wages—the average car wash attendant makes $11.49 per hour. She wonders what the dark-haired attendant might purchase with $11.49. His hair seems healthy, his hands seem youthful, and she thinks his name might be like hers (or how hers used to be) if his mother had chosen to reduce him to his most obvious quality.

Bruno buys eight caramel-filled candy bars for $11.49. Bruno buys a small piece of land near the car wash, a small square of it. He stands on the square with one foot; he has a strong core to balance, and he switches feet every few hours.

Get off my land, he could look at them and yell, *this here is private property.*

Van coughs and the phlegm makes itself known. Her nose is closed. The forest-green 540i is now brown and forest green, and the attendant, Bruno, seems more attractive than she had initially thought. Van removes all of her yellow hair, dry and brittle, but long, from the orange sweater. She watches Bruno notice this despite the layers of dirt covering the car. Van's sore purple nipples don't show through the orange sweater, but they are there, they both know this is so.

BENDING

On a crowded train underground, I refused to give my seat to a woman cradling a baby. I left her standing with the baby close to her breasts. Together they swayed.

The area outside moved fast, until it didn't. The train didn't shift again for three minutes. Then seven minutes, then twenty-five, stuck underground, and someone decided to light a cigarette. For thirty-seven minutes the smoke filled us. We couldn't see the culprit though we searched for him. It was so crowded that some people touched the ceiling to keep their balance. Their hands were up, high up, their wrists bent back. Hands up, as if waiting to be selected in a classroom, as if waiting for authority, and cotton shirts pulled over all the nostrils, the chemical compounds, the chorus of coughing. A cry.

Everyone was bending their knees, upon the woman's small breasts the baby was bending its knees, and the smoke played with us. Someone, a woman, yelled to the unknown culprit: *Put out that goddamn thing right now, or I swear, I swear to God.*

HAINT

I couldn't explain, but the candle burned for longer than usual and the smell of peonies persisted. The flowers leaned a little more to the side; the painting was more purple or more morose. The feathers didn't move at all. The red light that signaled the television's rest was piercing, a bright red light that even the black tape couldn't cover. The corner held the shadow of clothing and made shapes with them. The fan didn't cool the skin; it only made noise. The pillows were uncomfortable; I found no ease in them. The white sheets seemed cleaner than ever before. The mirror was clean too and held no discernible streaks.

My eye pencils were consumed. My head was covered with diamonds. I couldn't balance; the equilibrium couldn't be kept. I wore a braid down my back and a trench coat. Or a white turtleneck, leather pants, platform heels; things I had never worn. The hair that came free of a braid moved as if in wind, even if there was no wind. My nails were painted a purple/blue, and the smell of lime was everywhere.

In the kitchen I found things already sliced into neat circles and waiting on a plate. In the garbage I found things. I found pickled daisies, lockets, coarse salt, whole grains, swans, wooden chairs, and mortadella. The bed was dented in inexplicable places; the ceiling became vaulted.

The crown moldings remained the same and I was glad.

The olives, which once fell perfectly into the crease of my hand, no longer fit. The olive pits tasted of bubble gum. The coconut chunks were too tender; the chairs became flammable. The ice wouldn't melt, not after a day or after an hour. I dreamt of air balloons. The prescribed pills were more effective; they eased my anxiety and my depression.

The automobile changed models. It got me where I needed to be, but the model changed, and every time I drove the amenities differed, the buttons shifted, the heated seats came and went. One day my legs would be warmed, the next day they would not.

The hedges grew too quickly, even though they were trimmed every week. The condiments didn't expire; the canned foods didn't expire. The soup came with a sunny side egg on top, superb. The cherry tomatoes were not red but yellow. Everything that went in my mouth was covered in honey, thyme, fennel seeds, maple syrup, ground ginger, lime. The knives and the pizza cutter were sharpened, they cut through anything, they cut through my left thumb, I felt it slice through completely and felt the blood bubble up. I pressed. I put all the pressure I could on it. The skin was flapping around. I washed the dishes with one hand; with one hand I dried the dishes. I ate the yellow cherry tomatoes, and everything was sharp.

POOL

The seasoning must go under the skin, it must get under your nails, Mya said. The wind had picked up and was moving the back of her taupe shirt, or the beige shirt, waving it around and filling it up like a balloon. Beige or taupe, but it was her hair moving around her forehead that stood out, too short to be incorporated into a ponytail. The lights moved across her face and I was hardly listening to this suggestion, about the seasoning going under the skin of the animal. I couldn't focus on it, it's true, I wasn't listening. I was looking at her forehead and at the hair around the edges, keen.

I did that for a while. Noticing how it moved around her forehead. What I heard when I began to listen again were instructions for making rose water—*pull the petals off like an artichoke, in a saucepan combine water and these lost petals, boil them, simmer them*. This interested me so I listened to the instructions, *when ready*, Mya said, *the water will be tinted, light, the petals will be worn.* When she spoke her tongue came between her teeth; she had a lisp.

When we walked into the condo it was lit up in a red light, she preferred the red lighting, *it helps with my eyes,* Mya said. So in her condo everything was awash in red, even that tongue between her teeth and the teeth themselves above and below it. She placed rose water on her temples. *The red light prevents damage to the retina, it produces collagen, it also helps you think more acutely,* she said.

A manila envelope was near her right hand as she spoke, with a phone number and a name scrawled on it, something that began with an M; I couldn't tell because the writing slanted and was mostly illegible. There were also circles on the envelope, a tornado of black ink, as if someone had tried a pen that was almost empty or dried from disuse.

On the television there was figure skating. The woman at the center of the rink wore green. Her left leg slid behind her right leg and the right foot was out in front of her, then it moved behind her left ankle, an impossible thing in the air, a fall. I'd missed more of Mya's words while watching the ice. Mya continued, explaining something about elevators, about how they're not completely closed or sealed, how air always gets in, which reminded me of a red elevator I often used when I'd lived elsewhere. Mya continued on.

There were dollar bills on the kitchen table. I noticed it from my place on the couch, rubber bands around stacks of dollar bills. I was curious about the money: What was it for? Then she was pointing at her breasts, and I listened to everything she said about them.

The rug had flowers in it. I didn't know what type of flowers, but they were large and white against the black rug. On the walls near the baseboards someone had drawn something—an incoherent design with black markers, wild, as if made by a child. There was dust down there, on the baseboards and on the wooden furniture. There was dust on her perfume bottles. This was not how I would imagine taking care of a home. Mya was speaking about a blow dryer, something I wasn't interested in. I thought of the palm trees moving in the humidity and a backdrop of balconies, hundreds of balconies, and of my hips burning from the sun.

It smelled sweet in her condo, honey. Outside, there was a swimming pool. The floor was a red clay set against the white border and the blue of the water, and in the pool some children were swimming unsupervised while Mya said, *the cheese was all over the bedding that day*, and though I didn't understand what she meant I didn't ask her to explain. The ladder could be seen under the water, and four stainless step pads.

A cross hung in the middle of the room where we sat. There was dust on the cross. Mya believed in Jesus, and in all his agony he watched us. The red light was on Jesus. I watched myself in the mirror. Mya continued on, and I adjusted my pants, unbuttoning them to give relief. In the condo she spoke of the reasons why she wouldn't cook, that it was *too hot to cook, and anyway when is the last time we went out, we should go out, we deserve this*, she said. So we went out, out of the red condo, and I observed the couple next to us. They were unmoving, his hands in his lap and the woman's hands on her phone. They didn't speak. It was the kind of interaction I wished we could have, a quiet and melancholic intimacy. But Mya spoke and spoke. The food was subpar. The staff was efficient and kind. Mya did not pay attention to them in any way; she didn't thank them when they refilled her glass of water. She spoke with her mouth open.

Mya burped in her hand. We paid the bill. At the pool, the children were gone. We shared a bottle of cabernet. It was late and no one was around. We put our feet in the water. The plastic container held our leftovers. Mya talked. We'd had shrimp, yucca, and rice in a garlic sauce.

The water was lit up by the lights inside the pool. The smell of chlorine. I wanted to get in but didn't say so. We were dry. The shrimp, yucca, and rice in the plastic take-out container kept us company. I could see the window of Mya's condo above us, the cross hanging on the wall, the ceiling fan moving almost imperceptibly, the redness all over. I watched the water move around our legs and I didn't engage anymore. I didn't nod in agreement or say yes yes, right, right, yes. Mya continued, and as I moved to get up she kept on, telling me how the next person would not be so lousy. I dried my legs against the length of my skirt and she said that no one was worthy of her, *unworthy*, she said, and as I turned my body away she repeated many times over how anyone should be so lucky.

HANGNAILS, AND OTHER DISEASES

1.

The loss of a language is dizzying. There are times when it's lost. Words cannot be found and they will not come. It's a blurry loss, sorrowful. Like the word for *grapefruit*. Yesterday, it was lost. Popillo? Popello? The word escapes me. To be bilingual is to be in a state of recovery.

2.

It was in Paris where I broke my tooth, the lower left second molar, while chewing the bread with the engraved cursive P upon its breast. It was our first trip together as adults. The laugh lines were settling in.

We had woken up early to walk there in the rain. I liked the unevenness of the cobblestone, how I tripped at almost every step and how loud the cars sounded as they approached. We walked in the rain.

The woman at the counter of the shop didn't look at you. The woman at the counter asked if I wanted the whole loaf or the half, she directed the question at me as if she knew I would pay. I was distracted by her immediate knowledge of us, and by the smell of the dough rising out of sight, which reminded me of my father's calloused hands, how they could be abrupt, but also subtle. He used the abrupt hands or the subtle hands to make gnocchi.

I didn't understand her French, so she made wide shapes, and then I understood but could not decide between the two choices, the whole or the half, and you didn't help, so I told her yes, *oui*, the whole loaf, and made a circular shape with my fingertips. I carried it home, you were upset at the price of the whole loaf, so your hands were free to swing at your sides, the bread weighed one kilogram. The soft rain wet our hair.

3.

My hair is surrendering. The strands remain in whatever position they are left in: folded under the tension of an elastic band, or the shape of a pillow, or a hat, or the short fingers of someone new. The surrendering hair is curly and dark, like a lake that will never drain into another body.

Your hair might be more voluminous than mine, perhaps with a thin line of gray around the arch, it might still smell the same and your hair might move like it used to.

4.

Dermatophagia: from the Greek: skin, eating. The habit or compulsion of eating, biting, or enjoying one's own skin, most commonly on the fingers. They were often waiting near your lips, your long fingers. In any photo where you faced the camera there would be your hairline, the pupils, the curved nose, hands, hands, a birthmark, and the one finger between your lips as if amputated, the long neck.

You would grab all the skin available, speaking between bites, mouthfuls of it, skinning. Teeth gnawing, lips twisted to the left or to the right. The inside of the mouth would be marked with the missing skin, and you would run your tongue against it sometimes. From the outside it looked like a wave, and your cuticles were marked red.

5.

To add or subtract or multiply means to count in another language.

6.

As a child you studied the anatomy of butterflies, like Nabokov, you studied the intricacies of wings, their dotted red-orange patterns, the elbows and curves of their genitalia—lamella: liplike element; corpus bursa: component of genital duct; aedeagus: the penis.

It had never before occurred to me that butterflies had genitalia. And they were only beautiful to me if seen from afar. But you liked them close.

Small creatures that come from eggs—I suffered near them. Moths, and bees, and mosquitoes, and flies. It was their inability to be polite as they approached and their persistence.

I sleep with pillows draped over my head.

7.

The fear of belly buttons, omphalophobia. You hated belly buttons, and you hated the sounds of dry cotton being manipulated, of cotton swabs in ears, or of tissues in nostrils, or anyone who would touch your belly button with cotton.

8.

We kissed only once, in my bedroom and behind the bed. We were playing hide and seek and we both hid in the same place, so there was no seeking, no one sought anyone else. The synthetic toys were spread everywhere, spread all over the porcelain tile, the sun leaning against the window, and the coldness of your hands on my cheeks as you held me in place.

I've told all the people since to place their hands on my cheeks, *not like that, like this, yes, here, just so.*

9.

It was your cousin Valter that pointed out the differences in our skin tones and in our hair, how you had a shorter torso, a flat behind. My hair was overwhelming, he said.

Valter, his name means ruler of the army.

I had never cared about these details before he mentioned it. We were on a blue boat when he mentioned it.

The jellyfish[§§] poisoned me that day, stinging my left inner thigh. With their busy arms they poisoned me. Some-

---

§§ Jellyfish don't need a respiratory system, and some cannot detect images, only light. Their skin is thin, thin-skinned, mesoglea, and they use muscles to contract and to expand, the most efficient of swimmers.

one's urine was used to stop the burning, maybe Valter's, though it is medically unadvised.

10.

The word comes abruptly, like the light and the sheep and the fields from the window of the train, the word for grapefruit, there it is, pompelmo.

11.

Sometimes I want a moment of recklessness, or something altogether new. I watch myself cry in the bathroom mirror. I like to watch myself cry in a mirror, or in a window, in a broken television, in any reflective surface, really.

12.

My favorite view is a body when it is hanging on a bed, breasts swimming toward the arms, the arms down at your sides, armpits with forgotten hair, and the ribs, arched bone. There are usually a dozen, they curve and wrap around, connecting to the spine, the sternum, there are ribs that float. Did you know? Floating ribs. And the knees, of course, largest joint, we take the largest joint for granted—

the cartilage, the fluid and meniscus; the knees touching, close and touching, then the thighs, and again the ribs, the ribs.

13.

On the third bite of bread my tooth cracked hard and the pain was only secondary to the violence of the split. The second molar on the left succumbed. Only this second molar. I no longer had the third molar or the wisdom tooth, empty spaces, the teeth already removed and made blank years earlier in a white room (fluorescent) by an American dentist who did not listen with his gloved plastic fingers.

14.

In the glass apartment you made me two plates of pasta: la carbonara and aglio, olio, e peperoncino (with too much garlic). You forced me to eat them one right after the other. Your son watched as you watched me eat. It did not occur to me that I was eating alone.

I ate them both, one right after the other.

15.

I have never received a love letter, so I wrote one to myself. It is quite somber, brief. It's not very kind, but it's true. It ends: *I valued you the first time. I don't want to say more.*

16.

I feared falling on my chin, a kidnapping, or slipping and hitting my temples, smoke inhalation. You were only afraid of flying or of falling.

I have flown many times over the Atlantic. While others watch movies, I follow the illustrated map. And the cars that can be seen making right turns outside the scratched windows, plus the lights, the homes, tiny homes; the people are there beneath. I chose the window seat. You preferred middle seats, aisles. We have flown many times over the Atlantic.

On a plane you brought along important items: stones, seashells, jewelry. Hard objects that might not disintegrate so easily. You explained your reasoning:

> *someone could find them in my pockets, and identify my remains. Relatives could come near the crash site, the place where I was lost. They could wait between briefings to be told how my body parts may be hard*

to locate, how there would only be fragments, little
pieces of bone, teeth, or hard objects, stones, seashells,
jewelry.

17.

Two teeth, numbers one and nineteen, were removed with local anesthesia. It was fast, but full of pressure. The surgeon held my head like a basketball (one hand on the left side, one in the middle) and his forearm lay on my temple; his chest was on my neck.

Cracking, pushing, pulling hard. When it was out, the pain was gone. The surgeon would not suture the wounds, so the gums were left wide and gaping. I ate carefully. My nails were painted red and my gums were left open.

18.

The grapefruit was never my favorite, but you ate it whole, so I ate it whole too. The sour juice followed us around.

19.

I traveled to an island. There was a window from which I could only see the sea. The sheets smelled of something sour and clean. I swam. I ate apricot jam and paccheri with pieces of branzino. I took photos of myself in mirrors to pass the time. I cried in the mirror. I read books.

I traveled to the philharmonic. I was unprepared for the temperature so I purchased a sweater on the street. I did not know the language and there were 2,500 parks. I ate pistachios by the river. I rode the train. It was windy, and when I walked my hat wouldn't stay in its place. The cab I took smelled of maple syrup. I ate bread with vegan butter, castelvetrano olives, and goat cheese with black pepper. Leek and pumpkin soup. I drank red wine. I walked fast to catch a train, a tram, or a bus. In my room I undressed and dressed again. On the eighteenth floor I dressed, and I brushed my hair. I attended a concert. Everyone wore black, and I moved past the crowd wearing black. I felt the buzz from the wine.

20.

Misophonia, or the hatred of sound, for example the sound of one's own voice. We hear ourselves with the vibrations of eardrums and vocal cords, and airways. I heard my own voice when it echoed during a long-distance phone call. You were on the other end and my voice was thin. That day you called me with the worst news, the news that we would not speak again, never again, I heard my own voice.

21.

I never found the part of my tooth that chipped, it fell from my hands as I ran into the bathroom, and the floor was wet. I grabbed the sink to keep my balance. I searched but I could not find it.

LA GENOVESE

le cipolle, tagliate e poi immerse nell'acqua e sale, sale fino
per levare l'acidità. A fuoco lento, per un'ora con le carote e
il sedano, dopo quaranta minuti la carne, poi, aggiungi due
dita di vino, fai sfumare, e un altro pizzico di sale, l'olio ex-
travergine, gira, coprilo, sempre a fuoco lento. Scoprilo per
un'ora, girando piano piano fino a che diventa una crema,
ziti grandi, scegli qualche pasta doppia, dopo un po', o dopo
tre ore—no, ricorda, non serve altra acqua, le cipolle cac-
ciano loro l'acqua,

The onions, cut up and immersed in water and salt, fine salt, to remove any acidity. On a low flame, and for one hour, simmer the onions with the carrots and the celery, and after forty minutes add the meat (whatever piece of meat, any piece of meat, but it should be red), add a drop of wine (red), let it evaporate, add another pinch of salt, extra virgin olive oil, stir it, cover it, always on a low flame. Remove the lid, stirring until it becomes something new, and after a while, or after three hours, it is done.

CATCALLS

We tumbled. We held each other. We wore orange and browns, and her box braids were teal. A white car rode by, the wheels something shiny. The rims were something someone had invested in. They yelled from the car and then the white car pulled off. We didn't know what the man had hoped to threaten. We ignored it all; we scratched each other's scalps.

On the stoop, we waited for the dishwasher to complete its cycle. We counted each other's stretch marks. The rain clouds were coming close and the temperature was dipping down. We wore masks made of each other's faces. No one noticed this change—our families hadn't noticed and the man in the white car hadn't noticed.

The grass came up high and needed to be cut. The weeds were everywhere. A blue bicycle lay on its side. We wore gold jewelry around our necks. We wore gloves that came to our upper arms. It was the end of summer; we wore long-sleeve see-through dresses, or sleeveless white dresses that came up to our necks, orange and brown dresses. Our bodies were mostly covered.

Everyone stopped to look at us—at our attire, at our hair, and at the way we tumbled into one another. No one looked at our masked faces; our masked faces were identical to our mothers' faces. If someone spoke to us we didn't stop what we were doing, we didn't care to show respect or a sign of listening. As soon as the catcalls were gone we were at it again, wrestling or sitting still.

The rough steps hurt our legs. We talked it through and decided to move, to go for a walk around the block. We went as we were. People catcalled us as we made our way around the block. It took us time to navigate through all the people in the street and all the objects in the street. We navigated these threats, these solicitations, these jokes, the chatter. We smiled at some men because they seemed violent, and we were quiet with men who seemed only to be joking. *I'm joking*, they told us, and we took them at their word.

Someone threw a broom at us when we misread them. We had done everything right but it was no use. The broom just missed our legs.

If we saw someone we recognized from the neighborhood we waved. We didn't speak to anyone; we didn't offer them solace. We only offered stillness, our ears or our smiles. For the last half mile we raced. I lost, and I let her go up ahead of me. We were a few feet apart, but without our proximity chaos ensued.

At the crosswalk we met and the chaos subsided. We reached the stoop again, the blue bicycle. The masks were difficult to breathe in. We watched the light change across the street. Men called from their cars (blue, metallic, pearl); someone moved their hand in a way that suggested masturbation. A bus went by and someone with a nose ring looked at us from the window seat. We left the stoop, we stepped off the curb—a hydrant had been undone, and we walked in its path. Someone's unopened package had been abandoned in the hydrant's path, and the bottom of the cardboard was overcome, ruined.

CONSTELLATIONS

after Lorna Simpson

The women cut with sharp heavy shears, defunct, found images, pieces from *Ebony*, *Jet*, the editorial breasts hanging, and the splintered knowing, drinking peppermint tea, strands stiff with hairspray or stiff with the cosmos, architecture or the earrings, pearls, nail beds and shoulder blades, 19 x 14 gems on gray paper, glued, the body touched with water-soluble paint, an ether, the eyes fixed toward the lens, or the one eye fixed and the other loose, centerfold, on page 119 the plucked eyebrows and on the same page a smile, stiff hair set ablaze, the roof collapsing, save $7.

IN THE SAND, THE NONCONFORMITY OF WOMEN WHO ARE VIOLENTLY SHUSHED

She removed the burgundy three-piece suit filled with the day's sweat. She removed her shoes and her socks. She watched the others do the same. She adjusted her breasts, which were askew. She felt the wind as it punctuated her skin, her arms. She thought of John, and of his hair, which moved like the wind moves. She had discarded her family for him, but John couldn't keep his mouth away from other nipples, pink nipples. Someone she didn't recognize asked her if she was afraid of what was to come—*no*, she told them, *I'm only afraid of drowning, I'm not afraid to wait.* The person she didn't recognize didn't seem satisfied and they moved away. There were hundreds of them, mothers, and they lined up on the side of the river. In their underwear, their bras. They turned the suits inside out and placed the blue pants, the gray socks, the ivory vests, the burgundy jackets, the floral lapel pins, and the silk pocket squares in the water. They were leaving the suits; their hands had bled from pricking them with needles. They were leaving; it was their duty to do so. Some of them cried. They made their way to the mountain, even though they knew it would be gone soon, in 51,276 years. The wind was cutting it down every day, every day it got a little bit smaller.

THE ETHICS OF PIRACY

When I was young, a white male doctor held my face while numbing my left eye with anesthetic drops. My hair pressed down under his palm, under his wedding band. He injected the Triamcinolone into the sclera, and into the brown skin around the eye, the most delicate skin, *look up look up* he always said. *Look up.* He was telling me how bad my eyes were getting, that I would need more surgery soon and that I should be more aggressive with the Durezol drops, the Prednisone, Mycophenolate, Methotrexate, by mouth, and the Humira injection into the left thigh. That he expected me to take it all more seriously, *do you want to go blind?* He asked this with a tone that didn't seem appropriate. I didn't respond, because he continued speaking soon after, there was no time to tell him, *no, no I don't.* He had eight kids, and his wife didn't wear makeup. He told me, *I don't really care for makeup on women, my wife, she doesn't wear it.* He spoke quickly and I sometimes sped up the way I spoke to mimic him. I stopped wearing makeup. When I visited we would move into several rooms. He would put the yellow dye in my veins and immediately warn me about how my pee would be yellow. *Not the normal yellow of a dehydrated person, but highlighter yellow. Yellow yellow,* he always said, even though we had done this many times. I already knew. He stared at my arms while he took the anagram. He never asked how to pronounce my name. I followed him into another room. He had a certain walk, hips forward, feet slightly turned in. A swaying walk. I copied him sometimes as I followed behind, to pass the time. We moved into a third examination room. I sat across from him. There was a pause in this part of our interaction; I think he expected me to elaborate. So we would sit in this silence. It was a long time to sit that way, staring at each other. He looked very serious whenever he finally spoke, he would tell me the news, that *the eyes were getting worse, the medicine hasn't been taken as directed, by mouth. There's a lot of inflammation in the back of the eye, and in the front,* he said, *and it's not looking good.* I noticed that his eyes were two different colors. The left eye, my left as I was facing him, was slightly darker than the right, my right. I had never noticed this. *If you don't take better care of the eyes, you will eventually lose them,* he always said. *Your eyes will be cut out.* Before leaving I took an object with me from his office. Sunglasses. I left without scheduling the next appointment. When I was young, after a doctor's appointment, I would walk to the YMCA pool. I would arrive sometime in the afternoon. I would change in the locker room. On one of those occasions, my navy-blue one-piece was missing. The entire gym bag had been forgotten, probably in the farthest corner of my bedroom. I asked people in the locker room if they could spare a bathing suit. Some of them didn't look at me, and others looked at me but did not respond. I decided to swim with what I had—panties, the high-waisted white cotton panties with black dots, and the light-gray translucent bra. I took off my things. I took off my t-shirt and my bracelets, the gold studs my grandmama had given me, my rings. I moved toward the pool in my white-and-black cotton underwear, in my see-through bra, high up on my toes, a relevé. I used to like the smell of chlorine. I sat poolside only for a moment, my bare thighs on the tile. My feet touching the cold water. I went in. I floated. The people swimming (three women, one man) looked lonely. I floated and thought about my eyes. I looked at the horrible lonely bodies. I thought about a man telling me that I could go blind, about how a man pressed his hand down against my hair, how some men might have a lighter brown eye and a darker brown eye. When I got out of the pool, I removed the wet panties, the wet bra. I threw them away in the nearby garbage. When I was young, I used to avoid the mirrors, but that day I caught a glimpse of myself. I don't want to say what I thought of it now. I got dressed. I put on my pants but left them unbuttoned: the turtleneck, the rings, and the stud earrings. My damp hair wet my shoulders, which dripped down to my lower back and eventually to my thighs and down my calves. After the pool, I walked. I walked for a long time and cannot remember what I thought about. I can't remember the temperature outside, the season, or even how many blocks I strode or any of the stores I might have entered. I remember only the discovery of my wallet being gone, dropped somewhere between the doctor's office and the pool, or between the pool and where I found myself then. I cried for a few minutes on the sidewalk. People bumped into me from behind. It was rush hour. The third wallet lost. I didn't have the patience or energy to retrace my steps, I couldn't say why. I decided to remove things again: the pants, to remove my shirt, and my rings, my earrings. I placed them against the remnants of a burned chair. It seemed like the right thing to do. It seemed I did not need these items as I walked to the Holland Tunnel, through its entrance and directly along the Holland Tunnel, smelling of chlorine. It took me one hour and thirty-six minutes to walk its length. On the evening news they called me *The Tunnel Lady*. There was a documentary made about me, edited with bystander cellphone footage, a short film, only twelve minutes long. A man and I recently watched the film together. Before it began, the words "Pirating is not a victimless crime" flashed across the black screen. We couldn't get past this warning, a seemingly insignificant part of the picture, and we rewound it to watch it again. I pressed pause; the writing was white and bold against a black background. We laughed hard when we saw it. Still laughing, his braids covered his face when he said, *but I don't think there are true victims. No one dies from pirating, the production companies make billions, trillions, what comes after trillions? What are the ethics of piracy?* "Digital theft harms the economy" the film told us in smaller writing underneath, always white. More laughter, we couldn't stop laughing: it was almost like cough-ing or speaking, using the larynx, the lungs, an exhalation of air. We pressed play with our thumbs, both of our thumbs on the button, his and mine—it's quite difficult to press a button with another person. Finally the film began: we saw someone walking, walking through the Holland Tunnel. A woman. She seemed young and she walked naked between the traffic. Her body was long, her knees and elbows ashy, she wore sunglasses. This film was not edited well, it seemed uneventful, but the woman was moving at a good pace and we knew she would make it to New Jersey. There was no score set to the film, only the honking and nothing else. Sometimes she moved slowly, other times she moved into a jog. *There are two tubes under the Hudson River*, I explained as the film continued, *an east-west mechanical ventilation, with fans that blow wind around, and something, something changes the air down there, so that the, um, the carbon mon-oxide from the car exhausts doesn't asphyxiate anyone, so it doesn't suffocate any of the drivers.* We paused the film, our two thumbs pressing, the woman frozen in her walk, her long arms swaying. And the striking breasts, filled and fro-zen. And he asked, *but how do they make the tunnel, with tubes underwater? You can't control water.* I didn't give him a response, I pressed play with my thumb, the right thumb, and I didn't wait for his thumb. The woman was walking again, she didn't have time to waste—with her sunglasses on and with her desolate arms swinging.

APPENDIX

I. BREATHE: Breathing, and it's already done. The running was over, my legs were tired from it. It was my whole body, my lower back especially, and my legs, all of the individual parts of my legs were sore. The fatigue was not only physical but mental, it arrived and instructed me to sleep. That's what I did, for many days, and when I awoke I was still tired. There is such a thing as too much sleep, and I had had too much of it. I can't explain what has already happened; it's already done and needs not be repeated. If you missed it, I'm sorry. But this thing, it's done and my body aches from it.

II. SPACE HEATER: What we wanted was the sun, but it hadn't come. We turned on the space heater, to get things going and to know something of warmth and comfort. The water bottle was almost emptied; I cannot say what happened to its contents. Under my arms there's a sign that deodorant is needed, not a smell but a feeling. Sticky.

III. MIRRORS: What of mirrors? Not the mirrors in our homes, not the clean ones, but those outside, those located in the common spaces. What of these reflective surfaces that cannot complete their intention? What of them? How can we help them? When I'm out in a place that holds mirrors and people, I'm disgusted by these surfaces. Grease and time and contact have stained them, burdened them, they are dented or scratched. They are set against colors that cannot complement them; they reflect individuals who do not brush their bodies with washrags. They reflect the tiles that need replacing, the bottles of top-shelf liquor. The bathroom stalls are sometimes made of stainless steel, bought with the hope of imperviousness to rust or bacteria, and these bathroom stalls, these partitions are sometimes reflective. They are mirrored and they are scratched up like hell.

IV. A THEFT: Everything that is reflective is mostly on a car, a white car or an orange car. And in the corners of these spaces, a petal, a petal or when you move closer it's an arm.

An arm or something. Or when you leave your bag behind on a bench, or a wall that can be sat upon, what do you do with that loss? A bag that can hold almost everything, all the things that necessitate movement? There's so much that can fit in a bag that doesn't even belong in a bag, and therefore the loss of such items can be profound. A straw bag can be lifted from your shoulder without notice.

V. GARLIC SUPPLEMENTS: Vitamins feel like a scam. We take them, but we dislike the process of purchasing them or considering them. There is even a garlic pill, to give you the effects or the nutrients of garlic without eating the garlic itself (to increase antioxidant enzymes and reduce oxidative stress). They give you the things we can find on our own. They give you things we already own, the garlic buds are right in the kitchen, turn the corner, around that corner, they're hanging from the ceiling.

VI. GO FISH: And ice, in a package or in hand, an object that exists but is also fleeting, at any moment it can be around your ankles. Ice or even a sculpture on the wall of a nondescript avenue, with everything around it seeming so regular that the contrast can be jarring or unwelcome. Fish on ice, or how when they've emerged from their place they are bent into a blue bucket, sometimes flapping, always gasping. Fish, or an octopus that looks deflated and ungodly in the blue bucket. To fish, to go fishing is to say something with the body, there is a certain respect but also a longing to kill these creatures and fold them into a blue bucket. The water helps to ease the violence. *Go fish*, she says, and I pick up the card from the pile in the center.

VII. MORE GARLIC: The purple garlic waits on paper plates, and the bulbs (seven to nine) are wondrous. The lamp and the vase surround the purple garlic. The body (which aches, still) surrounds it. And there's a division in the grocery store that is evident: the organic produce is divided into smaller and more fragrant portions. The rest of us pick up the regular lemons, the non-organic lemons, and know we aren't getting what we need, though they taste fine and the juice flows. I look for the people who approach what is organic; I set a place for them at the table. With the cloth napkin and the utensils. The fine utensils are pure silver. Have you ever cleaned utensils that had been stored away for long? It's a process much like fishing, there is a violence to keeping things in disuse for so long, and then fetching them out, and then cleaning them in a rush, killing them. The guests are arriving and there isn't that much time to polish the forks.

VIII. TANGLED NECKLACES: When the hips protrude it's a sight, and we don't mean to look but we do. Our aunt who is shaped like a mountain got these looks and she's handed them around. Her bowed legs when seen in heels were like a bastion or a lighthouse. What does it mean to hold a face with both hands and to spread a face, to see it without time or memory, or wine? Two necklaces tangled up, impossible to rescue but we pick at the knotted gold with our fingernails for they must be undone.

NOTES & ACKNOWLEDGMENTS

NOTES

"The Balcony" (p. 40): The verse about an extension cord, grape jelly, and hominy grits is a reference to the film *Ganja & Hess*, 1973.

"Three Months of Banana" (p. 50): The mentions of Muhammad Ali riding a horse in the streets of Harlem are from the film *Black Rodeo*, 1972.

"Forty-Seven Days Ago" (p. 70): In conversation with Sophie Calle's *Exquisite Pain*, 1984–2003; "Peach" (p. 93): In conversation with Calle's *The Giraffe*, 2012.

"There's D'Angelo's Gap" (p. 82): Paul Hunter directing D'Angelo is from *MTV Making the Video, Untitled (How Does It Feel)*, 2000.

ACKNOWLEDGMENTS

To Danielle Dutton and Martin Riker for seeing something in this work, my first work, and for shaping it. To Laurie Sheck who gave me encouragement, counsel, and consistent care. Gratitude to Rachel M. Simon, Ashley C. Ford, Val Vinokur, and Katie Kitamura. To my peers, the earliest readers of these stories, especially Leia Inji Carter and Yasmin Zaher (for the bees). To Asandele Sondiyazi, Callie Barrons, Luthfun Jui Nahar, Natalie Fletcher, Ruwa Alhayek.

To the women who have shared their hands: Tiffany Mellard, Jessica Sanchez, Courtney Wheeler, Vanessa Stair, Jenna Hanchard, Gabriela Suriel, Kendra Williams, Ilaria Carratù.

Clark Scully, for everything underlying and for the rest.

Alla mia famiglia, per la luce.

And to all the places that have kept me.

ABOUT THE AUTHOR

Giada Scodellaro was born in Naples, Italy and raised in the Bronx, NY. She holds an MFA from The New School. This is her first book.